MW01138928

Cover Design and Interior Format

FORTUNE'S
BRIDES
BOOK
SIX

Never Marry a Marquess

REGINA SCOTT

To the man I married—age is just a number, love is not counted in minutes. I will love you today, tomorrow, and always. And to the Lord, who knew exactly what I needed in a husband.

CHAPTER ONE

London, England, July 1812

Would she ever become accustomed to Society? Sitting in the hired coach, Ivy Bateman smoothed down the satin skirts of her evening gown, the color reminding her of clotted cream. Since her brother Matthew had been elevated to a hereditary knighthood for saving the prince's life, her world had changed. Where once she had spent her days keeping Matthew's house and caring for her younger sisters, now she entertained fine ladies over tea and promenaded in Hyde Park at the fashionable hour. In the evenings, she used to read a thrilling adventure novel by the fire before taking her weary body off to bed to dream. Now she sometimes didn't reach her bed before the sun was up. And she found herself dreaming of things she couldn't have.

"Stay by my side at the soiree," Miss Thorn advised from across the coach. "I will ensure we only converse with gentlemen Charlotte or your brother have already approved."

Ivy's younger sister, Daisy, wiggled beside her, her pale pink gown wrinkling against the padded leather seat. "That's no fun. What if a charming prince asks for an introduction? I'm expected to turn my back on him?"

"Alas, princes, charming or otherwise, are in short supply,

even for the earl and countess." Miss Thorn adjusted her long silk gloves. "And any fellow who approaches without an introduction cannot be a gentleman."

Daisy slumped, then perked up again. "But if you were to introduce him to us, that would be permissible? We can't help that Charlotte and Matthew are out of town."

Their brother and his bride were off on their honeymoon to the Lakes District. A shame Ivy couldn't have gone along, if only to escape the hubbub that was London as the Season wound to a close. But Matthew and Charlotte deserved time to themselves. Miss Thorn, who had introduced Charlotte into the Bateman household as an etiquette teacher, had offered to serve as chaperone in Charlotte's absence so Ivy and Daisy could continue the social whirl. After all, Charlotte and Matthew held out hope Ivy and Daisy would marry well. Ivy just wanted to survive the Season and retire to the quiet of the house, perhaps do some baking.

Simple, productive baking.

Miss Thorn probably didn't bake. She probably didn't worry that her hair was piled up properly or her gown was too simple either. The lavender silk with its rows of pleats at the hem was the exact shade of her eyes. Not a curl of her raven hair escaped the pearl-studded combs that held it in place. Still, the employment agency owner looked odd without her cat Fortune in her arms.

"I expect to know a number of the attendees," Miss Thorn allowed, and Daisy brightened, until she continued, "Most will be at least a decade older than you and happily married. But if I spot a likely gentleman, I will be sure to draw his attention. Just see that you ask him to call so that Fortune may give her blessing."

Fortune had an uncanny way of knowing whether a person was worthwhile. And to think she approved of Ivy.

The cat had been less approving of her sister, and Ivy couldn't help wondering if Daisy's impetuous nature wasn't to blame.

Now her sister puffed out a sigh. "Old people shouldn't be allowed to host events."

Ivy put a hand on her arm. "A decade older than sixteen is not so very aged. Besides, you know Lady Carrolton will host a lovely soiree in her new home. Remember her ball?"

"Yes," Daisy said. "But she's just a countess, and she's French. Matthew is friends with the prince. We should be moving in higher circles."

"This is quite high enough for me," Ivy assured her.

Daisy turned her gaze out the window.

Ivy caught herself smoothing her skirts again and forced her gloved hands to stop. She might feel uncomfortable in such glittering company as the earl and his wife, but Daisy only wanted more. At times, she reminded Ivy of their stepmother.

She must fight any association there. Mrs. Bateman was easily the most grasping, cruelest woman Ivy had ever met. Last they had heard, she had taken up with a wealthy Irishman and headed across the sea to his country. Ivy could only hope they never saw her again.

Miss Thorn gathered her fan. "Here we are now. Stay beside me, girls. We wouldn't want to be separated in the crush."

"*You* wouldn't want us to be separated," Daisy muttered.

Oh no. Ivy had been both mother and sister since she was twelve. She was not about to let Daisy slip away. She linked arms with her sister as soon as they alighted.

At times, she marveled at the differences between them. Ivy was tall and curvy. Daisy was a pocket Venus, the same curves poured into a much shorter stature. Ivy's hair was a sunny blond like their mother's, Daisy's a thick dark brown like their brother's and father's. The one thing they shared was a pair of walnut-colored eyes, but while Ivy tended to look at the world in wonder, Daisy viewed it in calculation.

But they both stared up at the house they were about to enter.

The Earl of Carrolton owned a London townhouse not far from Miss Thorn's on Clarendon Square. To honor his bride, he'd recently purchased and had renovated a larger house set off the square with its own gardens. Now the cream-colored stones glowed in the light of lanterns hung from the trees, and every window gleamed with candlelight.

"Beeswax," Daisy hissed to Ivy as they entered the marble-tiled hall and were directed up a set of sweeping stairs to the gallery. "You won't find an earl using tallow."

Indeed, no cost had been spared in decorating the house. The walls of the long gallery were covered in watered silk the radiant blue of the sky at sunrise, and oil paintings in gilded frames hung from the high ceilings. The teal and amber carpet sank under Ivy's satin slippers. She knew by the feel. She certainly couldn't see much of it, as the room was filled with London's finest, elbow to elbow, clustered in groups. Jewels flashed as ladies turned to greet friends. Laughter rode on the tide of conversation.

Daisy was craning her neck as Miss Thorn navigated them through the crowd. "I don't see Sir William." She had run into the rascal of a baronet more than once this Season and counted him a favorite. "But there are one or two fellows who might do."

"You may have them all," Ivy told her, stopping to allow Miss Thorn to speak to an old friend.

After they had been introduced and the two women were chatting, Daisy nudged Ivy. "Waiting for Lord Kendall, are we?"

The floor seemed to dip beneath Ivy's feet. "Of course not. We don't even know whether he'll be in attendance."

Daisy shook her head. "You can't fool me, Ivy Bateman. You want to be a marquessa."

"Marchioness," Ivy corrected her, and her sister grinned.

Ivy didn't waste her breath arguing. Daisy was certain

Ivy was smitten with the Marquess of Kendall. What lady wouldn't be? He was tall and elegantly formed, and he held himself as if he well knew his own worth. That sable hair curled back from a brow that spoke of intellect. His neat beard and mustache framed a mouth that offered compassion, suggested kindness. With a family as old as the Conquest and a fortune as deep as a well, he could easily have any lady he chose.

He would not choose her. Matthew might have been elevated, but Ivy was still the daughter of a millworker. She and Daisy were fortunate that their new sister-in-law, Charlotte, was the daughter of a viscount and sister to Lord Worthington, or they would likely never have set foot in a Society event. Even when they did, some refused to speak to them, staring at them when they passed as if aghast someone so common would be allowed admittance.

Still, the Countess of Carrolton had invited them, and, as the evening wore on, Ivy did her best to honor the lady. She accompanied Miss Thorn as she made her way around the room, greeted acquaintances, chatted about the weather, the shocking war America had declared on her mother country, and the latest fashion. Daisy lagged behind or forged ahead from time to time, but Miss Thorn or Ivy always managed to pull her back into their circle. Ivy knew Miss Thorn was keeping an eye on Daisy, but after caring for her sister since they'd lost their mother, Ivy found it difficult to remember she didn't have to be on her guard.

"Dare I claim this beauty for a promenade?" Sir William asked, gaze on Daisy and grin infectious.

Miss Thorn eyed him from his artfully curled blond hair to his polished evening pumps and inclined her head. "Once around the room, sir. I will be watching."

He bowed, then offered Daisy his arm, and the pair set off, Daisy preening.

"So that's where she's set her sights," Miss Thorn said.

Unease pulled Ivy's shoulders tighter. "She's clever. She'll learn her place."

The employment agency owner transferred her gaze to Ivy. "And what place would that be?"

Ivy felt the need to step back and promptly bumped into another lady. Turning to apologize, she had to raise her chin to meet the fierce gaze of the Amazon standing there.

"I do beg your pardon, Mrs. Villers," Ivy said, dropping her gaze.

"Miss Bateman," the lady intoned, sounding a bit as if she'd discovered a fly in her tea. "Miss Thorn."

"Mrs. Villers," Miss Thorn acknowledged. "Mr. Villers."

Ivy looked up in time to see the saturnine fellow at the lady's elbow raise a silver quizzing glass and examine Ivy and her chaperone through it.

"The Beast of Birmingham's sister, is it not?" he drawled.

"Sir Matthew Bateman's sister," Miss Thorn corrected him as Ivy's cheeks heated. "Miss Bateman, I don't believe you have met Mr. Villers. He is Lady Worthington's brother."

"And brother-in-law to the Earl of Carrolton," the fellow seemed compelled to remind her. "Good of you to come." He turned to his wife. "Isn't that dear Gregory waving us over, darling?" He offered his wife his arm, and the two sailed off, noses in the air.

"I do hope they don't go outside that way," Miss Thorn said. "If it was raining, they might drown."

Just then a footman approached them and bowed as well as he could among the crush. "I was asked to deliver this to you, miss." He offered Ivy a folded piece of parchment.

Ivy accepted it from him, mystified, then opened the note, aware of Miss Thorn's gaze on her.

I have made a cake of myself, the note read in Daisy's brisk hand. *Meet me in the library on the first floor, and don't bring Miss Thorn. I cannot face her now.*

"Trouble?" Miss Thorn asked.

Heart starting to beat faster, Ivy folded the note. "Just a friend reminding me of my duty. Will you excuse me? I won't be long."

Miss Thorn eyed her. Ivy willed her not to suggest she needed a chaperone, to remember they were at a party given by a trusted couple, to recall that Ivy was the reliable sister. Whether Miss Thorn heard Ivy's frantic thoughts or not, she inclined her head in consent, and Ivy hurried for the stairs.

The same footman directed her around the corner to the double doors of the library, and Ivy slipped inside. A single lamp had been left burning, so the corners of the room remained in shadow. By the golden light, she made out tall oak cases, offering row upon row of books she would at another time have been delighted to peruse. Indeed, the deep leather sofa before the black marble hearth invited her to linger and read.

"Daisy?" Ivy called, venturing deeper into the room. "Miss Bateman?"

Ivy turned to find the Marquess of Kendall standing in the doorway. The black of his evening coat and breeches emphasized his height. The lamplight picked out gold in his sable hair. He shut the door behind him and moved closer. "How might I be of assistance?"

There must be some mistake. He should not be here. She should not be here. Ivy edged around the sofa, away from him. "I need no assistance, my lord. I was concerned for my sister."

He frowned, following her. "Your sister, Miss Daisy?"

"Yes." She rounded the other end of the sofa and started for the door. "I must have misunderstood. Excuse me." She seized the latch and tugged.

The door refused to open.

Kendall watched as the pretty Miss Bateman pulled at the latch, color rising with each movement. She was such a cipher. The round face, the wide brown eyes, and her soft voice combined to make her appear sweet, uncertain, and full of amazement at the world. Yet there were moments when she exhibited an inner strength that surprised him. He had wondered whether she might be the woman he needed.

That woman had proven exceedingly difficult to find. Now that the Season was drawing to a close, his quest would become even more challenging. A marquess possessed of a decent fortune and an excellent family name ought to be able to locate a wife easily enough. But he didn't want a wife. He wanted a mother for Sophia.

Just the thought of his little daughter tightened his chest. Her mother had been the love of his life. It wasn't right that Adelaide had been taken so young, only the day after the birth of their daughter. Kendall never intended to give his heart again. How could he when it had gone to the grave with his wife?

But Sophia needed a mother, a woman who would cherish and guide her better than he could as her father. Oh, he knew not all mothers were so doting, but his father had assured him his mother had been. And so he had come to London in search of a bride among the ladies on the marriage mart.

He'd soon realized his error. The ladies suited to be a marchioness fell into one of two camps. Either they were idealistic and hoped for a love match, or they delighted in Society and would never have enjoyed rusticating in Surrey and raising another woman's child. He had learned Miss Bateman had guided her younger sisters and loved children, but he doubted she'd be content in the type of marriage he intended to offer.

Now she stepped back from the door with a frown. "It

appears to be stuck. Would you try, my lord?"

He offered her a polite smile and approached the door. Why was she dissembling? He'd received word from a footman that Miss Bateman requested his help on a matter of some urgency and would meet him in the library. He had not doubted the report. Since becoming acquainted with her family, he had been put in a position of offering assistance twice, most recently when her youngest sister had gone missing. That was the day he'd realized the strength inside her otherwise soft demeanor. Miss Bateman would have gone to the ends of the earth to see her sister safe.

Would that he found someone who cared so much about Sophia.

He took hold of the latch, gave it a good tug. Through the thick wood, he thought he heard a metallic rattle, but the door didn't budge.

"What's wrong?" Miss Bateman asked, fingers knitting before her creamy gown.

He yanked harder. Something creaked in protest, but still the door held firm. He released the handle and stepped back. "We appear to be trapped."

"How very inconvenient," she said.

Or was it convenient? He did not know her well, after all. Could she have set up this meeting to cry compromise? In the past, she had gone out of her way to avoid any situation that might be construed as intimate. Or did she, too, see her opportunities narrowing with the Season's end?

She could easily have taken advantage of the opportunity now. But she did not attempt to throw herself into his arms, begging for comfort in their circumstances. She went to sit on the sofa, back straight, head high. As he followed, he was not surprised to find her hands folded properly in her lap.

"What are you doing?" he asked.

Her gaze was on the barren hearth. "Waiting. Sooner or later Daisy or Miss Thorn will come in search of me."

Her faith was commendable. He leaned against the hearth. "I fear by that time the damage will be done."

She frowned, glancing up at him, lamplight shining in her dark eyes. "Damage?"

"To your reputation."

She drew herself up further. "You are a gentleman, sir."

He inclined his head. "Indeed I am. But the longer we are alone together, the quicker tongues will wag."

"Let them wag," she replied. "I have done nothing wrong, and I won't be pushed into apologizing."

There was that strength again. It called to him, beckoned him closer. He took a step without thinking.

The door rattled a moment before swinging open, and Miss Thorn strode into the room, eyes flashing like a sword. He'd once approached the woman for help with the idea that she and her cat were some sort of matchmakers. After all, the Duke of Wey, Sir Harold Orwell, Lord Worthington, and their host tonight, the Earl of Carrolton, had found brides through her. Now she looked like nothing so much as a winged Fury as she swept toward the sofa and held out one hand.

"Come, Ivy. Your sister is looking for you."

Ivy rose and hurried to her side. "Forgive me. The door jammed."

"Doors tend to do that when someone shoves a candelabra through the latches," she replied with a look in his direction.

He spread his hands. "May I remind you, madam, that I was trapped as well?"

"And may I remind you, sir, that I understand your purpose for being in London."

Kendall stiffened. He hardly wanted it known he sought a marriage of convenience. That would attract all the wrong kinds of interest.

She put an arm around Ivy's waist as if determined to protect her. "You will call on me tomorrow, Lord Kendall, and we can discuss reparations."

Ivy pulled away from her. "Reparations? But nothing happened, Miss Thorn. I promise you."

"I believe you," the lady replied, look softening. "But others may not. Think of Daisy's reception if you will not think of your own." She nodded to Kendall. "Tomorrow, my lord. I am usually receiving by eleven. I expect you then, with an offer."

And she pulled her charge from the room before he could decide just who was manipulating whom.

CHAPTER TWO

"But nothing happened," Ivy protested again once they were seated in the coach and headed for Miss Thorn's home. "We were alone less than a quarter hour."

"Lots of interesting things can happen in less than a quarter hour," Daisy put in helpfully. "A touch of hands, a kiss or two."

"Do you speak from experience?" Miss Thorn asked coolly.

"No," Ivy assured her with a look to her sister. "Daisy knows how to behave like a lady. We both do. That's why I have no intention of trapping Lord Kendall in this odious manner."

Daisy threw up her gloved hands. "He likes you; you like him. There's no *trapping* about it."

"Alas, a strategically placed candelabra says otherwise," Miss Thorn replied. "Who could have taken you in such dislike, Ivy, to put you in this untenable position?"

Mrs. Villers came to mind, but surely that lady had better things to do. And, feeling as she did about the inferiority of the Bateman family, she would hardly want to arrange matters so Ivy had a chance of becoming a marchioness. Ivy could think of no other person who disliked her. She was generally content to stay in the background. That sort of life did not lend itself well to making enemies. Though there was another possibility…

"I don't believe anyone dislikes me to that extent," she told their chaperone. "But perhaps the person was Lord Kendall's enemy, not mine. He is the one being forced to propose."

Daisy glanced between her and Miss Thorn. "Why are you both so Friday-faced? Ivy's going to marry a marquess. That's good for all of us."

"Perhaps," Miss Thorn allowed as the carriage drew up in front of her townhouse. "We can speak further in the morning. I asked Lord Kendall to call at eleven. I expect you downstairs at least an hour before, Ivy."

"Of course," Ivy agreed as they climbed out of the carriage.

Mr. Cowls, Miss Thorn's elderly butler, opened the door for them. His thinning white hair, usually pomaded into sleek lines about his head, now stuck out in all directions, and his black jacket hung crookedly on his tall frame.

"Master Rufus made an appearance," he said as if he noticed them staring.

"Is Fortune safe?" Miss Thorn demanded, hurrying past him into the entry hall.

"Miss Fortune appeared to enjoy his company the most," he replied, shutting the door behind them. "She is with Miss Petunia in the withdrawing room. The hound has been banished to the rear yard for the moment."

"I'm not going to ruin my gown to see to him," Daisy declared, marching for the stairs. "That dog is a disaster."

"I heard that!" Petunia, their youngest sister, stepped out onto the second-floor landing, the grey cat in her thin arms, hair far less mussed than Mr. Cowls's. "Rufus is a good dog. He just wanted to play."

Miss Thorn picked up her skirts and swept up the stairs behind Daisy, who continued to the chamber story, nose in the air as if she didn't see Petunia's glare. Ivy followed their hostess. Miss Thorn paused to examine her pet, who gazed up at her with copper-colored eyes.

"And how many scratches did Rufus sustain this time?" she asked Tuny, hand stroking the grey fur. Fortune lifted her chin as if to suggest she deserved a reward for her victory.

"Only a couple," Petunia acknowledged, offering their hostess the cat. "And it was his own fault for sticking his nose where he shouldn't."

"What am I to do with you two?" Miss Thorn asked her pet as she tucked Fortune closer. Then she raised her head to meet Ivy's gaze. "What am I to do with all of you?"

Petunia glanced between them, brown eyes turning down in concern. "Did something happen at the soiree?"

"Nothing of any import," Ivy assured her. "And I do wish we could cease discussing it."

"Very well," Miss Thorn said before calling down to her butler. "We are expecting an important visitor at eleven tomorrow, Mr. Cowls. Please see that the withdrawing room is set to rights by then." She dismissed Ivy with a nod.

Tuny followed Ivy up the stairs to the chamber story. Miss Thorn had given them each a bedchamber while they were staying with her, lovely rooms with box beds and pretty wallpaper. Ivy still didn't understand why they couldn't have stayed in their own house off Covent Garden. No one had questioned her ability to look after her sisters until Matthew had been elevated. They'd lived simply, quietly.

Frugally.

She shoved the thought away. At one of the balls they had attended, some had mentioned Charlotte's inheritance. Ivy wasn't sure of the amount or if it would stretch to cover any children Charlotte and Matthew might have. Matthew was already spending a pretty penny to have her and Daisy in Society. She must make the most of his kindness.

But that did not mean she had to marry the marquess.

"Something happened," Tuny said, catching Ivy's arm

before she could go into her bedchamber. "Who's coming tomorrow?"

Might as well let her sister in on the matter. Petunia had a way of finding things out and sometimes drawing the wrong conclusions.

"The Marquess of Kendall is calling," Ivy explained with a sigh. "Someone locked us in the Earl of Carrolton's library tonight, and now everyone is concerned about my reputation. It's a tempest in a teapot. He was a gentleman."

Tuny put her hands on her hips. "So, who locked you in?"

"No one knows," Ivy said. "Now, off to bed. I want a word with Daisy."

Tuny hugged her, then did as she was bid. Once she closed the bedchamber door, Ivy moved to Daisy's.

Her sister was sitting on the padded seat before the dressing table, waiting for Enid, Miss Thorn's maid, to assist her in undressing. She'd taken the pins from her hair to let it spill about her shoulders, the brown waves dark against the pink of her gown. Ivy came up behind her and met her gaze in the dressing table mirror. "Why did you do it, Daisy?"

Daisy's eyes widened. "Do what?"

"You know very well. I didn't tell Miss Thorn about the note, but you sent it. I recognized your hand. I wouldn't be surprised if you hadn't penned it before we left home. You led me to the library, and I suspect you somehow led Lord Kendall as well. Whose idea was the candelabra, yours or Sir William's?"

Daisy rearranged the brush and comb on the dressing table. "Sir William's. I just thought if I brought you and Lord Kendall together, nature would take its course. Sir William wanted to help it along. It was all in fun."

"Fun?" Ivy straightened. "Is that what you call forcing a man to propose to a woman he doesn't love?"

Daisy swiveled to face her. "Well, he wasn't going to do

it otherwise! And who says he doesn't love you? You are very lovable, you know."

Perhaps, for her family. But they were used to her. The other ladies in her sphere were so much more accomplished. Her new sister-in-law Charlotte was poised, confident. Daisy could talk to anyone, about anything. Too often, Ivy felt like the world was too big, or perhaps she was too small. How could a man of Lord Kendall's wealth and sophistication see her as a potential wife? *She* couldn't see herself that way.

"I have my strengths," she acknowledged to her sister. "But I am better suited to a family than the dictates of Society. Lord Kendall was wise enough to see that, until you forced his hand."

Daisy tossed her head. "If you ask me, you should thank me for bringing him up to scratch."

"I will thank you to keep out of my affairs," Ivy replied. "Or do you think I don't know my own mind? That I require help in choosing my future?"

Daisy had the good sense to drop her gaze. "No. You've always known what you were about, Ivy. I just think you aim too low when you could be so much more."

"And maybe I am content with what I am," Ivy chided her. "Besides, if Lord Kendall has decided we will not suit, I hardly want to push him into marriage."

"The more fool you, then," Daisy said, turning to her reflection and showing cheeks pinkening. "I wouldn't refuse a rich, handsome marquess if he proposed."

Perhaps she really was a fool, for that was exactly what she intended to do.

Kendall knocked at Miss Thorn's door at precisely eleven. He felt not the least trepidation, but that was nothing new. Feelings, of any kind, had been scarce since Adelaide had left him behind. At times, the world seemed distant, shrouded in mist, and he hadn't the energy to push through.

But for Sophia, he would move mountains.

Doctor Penrose's concern had only steeled his resolve.

"I have tried everything I can find," the young physician had explained as they'd talked outside the nursery a few weeks ago, listening to the nursemaid attempt to quiet Sophia's cries. "Various formulations of gruel, vigorous rubbing, poultices, even bleeding. She is not gaining weight, is not exhibiting the characteristics of a seven-month-old child. Such cases are all too common when the mother is taken from a child early. Your daughter is naturally frail, my lord. I fear without her mother she may not reach her first year."

Without her mother. Without a woman determined to love her. But Sophia's delicate nature, inherited from his dear Adelaide, would not cost her her life. He would make sure of it. He had come to London with a purpose, and though he made the trip to his estate in Surrey every few days, the physician having determined that travel might prove fatal for Sophia, he was not about to abandon his purpose now. This business with Ivy Bateman had forced his hand. But there was every possibility that she might be the woman Sophia needed.

Miss Thorn was waiting in her withdrawing room, perched upon a satin-striped sofa with her pet in the lap of her lavender-colored gown. Like the lady, the room was elegant, the epitome of good taste with its yellow and white appointments and collection of pottery displayed behind glass.

"Miss Bateman is not disposed to accept your offer," his hostess informed him, the cat's tail swishing lazily back and forth.

He paused in the act of sitting on the chair opposite

them. "You seem certain I intend to propose."

Her hands stroked the cat, who eyed him with a faintly chiding look. "You are a gentleman. And you seek a wife."

"Both true, but I did not trap Miss Bateman to gain one." He settled himself on the chair. The cat roused herself to slip from her mistress' lap and pace back and forth in front of him as if distrusting his motives.

"So you say," Miss Thorn replied. "Yet here we are. Do you intend to offer?"

He inclined his head.

She stood. "I'll allow her to meet with you, but I expect complete honesty about your proposal, sir. Ivy must know how little you offer."

Something tightened inside him. "Some would not consider a country estate, a townhouse, the funds to maintain them in style, and an ancient title paltry matters."

"Some choose to marry for love."

He flinched as the shame of the statement hit home. He had married Adelaide because they loved each other, their minds attuned to every little thing. They laughed at the same situations, finished each other's sentences. They enjoyed the same music, the same literature. Her health prevented her from taking part in his daily life, true. She had visited his beloved pavement room to admire the Roman mosaic once and spent the next three days sneezing. Still, he liked to think their love would have lasted through financial hardships, life's tragedies. Offering Miss Bateman less seemed a sacrilege, a betrayal of his vows.

He should apologize and go, return to his empty home, the void in his life.

Sophia. He was doing this for Sophia.

He drew in a breath. "I will tell Miss Bateman," he vowed. "I will put no pressure on her to accept."

"Very well," she said. Her gaze went to her cat. "See that he honors his promise, Fortune."

He was certain Fortune nodded in agreement.

He eyed the creature as Miss Thorn left the room and he waited for Ivy. She was a handsome animal, blue-grey coat interrupted by white around her neck and throat, as if she wore a cravat, paws tipped in white as if she wore gloves. She moved along the sofa with the languid grace of her breed, as if he was nothing and no one to her.

At the end of the sofa, she turned to eye him, watching him, unblinking.

"What do you see?" he asked.

He would not have been surprised if she had answered. But the door opened again, and Fortune bolted behind the sofa.

He rose as Ivy came into the room in a simple blue cambric dress. Morning dress, Adelaide had called it, the informal gown a lady wore in the privacy of her home. Ivy clearly had not set out to impress him. Still, did she realize the gown called attention to her curves and contrasted with the sunny blond of her hair, swept up properly behind her head? She took a seat on the sofa, and Fortune jumped up on the back, then slipped down beside her. Why was Ivy's gaze no less easy to ignore?

He took his seat. "Miss Bateman, thank you for receiving me."

"Of course," she said with a gentle smile. "We are friends."

Friends. Yes. Nothing said he could not be friends with a lady. "And as your friend, I must express my concern over what happened last night."

She raised a hand as if to stop him. "It was nothing. I wish you wouldn't refine on it."

"I find it difficult not to refine on it, though I agree that neither of us was to blame."

Her gaze brushed the door and returned to him. "Then let us continue as we were and say no more on the matter."

She was making it easy for him to walk out that door. His feet urged him to follow her implied suggestion. But he had been in London for three months and had found no other lady who even came close to being suited to the role he needed to fill.

Kendall leaned forward, determined to make his case. "Miss Bateman— May I call you Ivy?"

She blinked as if surprised, then pink crept into her round cheeks. "Yes, of course."

"Ivy, then. I do not know what you've heard of me, but I wanted to explain my purpose in London. I came to find a bride, a mother for my infant daughter."

A light sprang into her dark eyes. "You have a daughter?"

Sophia's face swam into his mind as he'd last seen her, the way she was so often: red-faced, eyes screwed shut, mouth open as she wailed. He could almost feel her pain, her confusion.

"Yes," he managed. "Her name is Sophia. Her mother, my wife, died in giving her life."

Her face sagged. "Oh, Lord Kendall, I'm so sorry." As if in full sympathy, Fortune abandoned her pose to cuddle closer, rubbing her head against Ivy's arm.

He swallowed the lump in his throat. This should not be so hard. He'd thought it through a dozen times. It was the only way. It was the right thing for Sophia. It didn't matter whether it was the right thing for him.

"It has been difficult," he acknowledged. "But I am convinced it is best to carry on. I believe I have much to offer a lady: comfort, ease, dare I say luxury?"

She dropped her gaze to the cat. "You are accorded quite the catch."

He grimaced. "You are too kind. But just as I know the benefits I bring to a marriage, I am fully aware of the deficits. I take a wife only for Sophia's sake. I do not intend to give my heart again. I will leave Sophia a generous bequest and provide amply for my wife. My title and lands will go to my younger brother or his son, should he have one."

She glanced up to regard him with a slight frown. "You

do not intend a true marriage?"

"Only one of convenience," he explained. "Though in my case, I might call it a marriage of necessity. My daughter is ill. She fails to thrive. We have tried everything our physician can devise, consulted with others around the country and the Continent. Still she struggles."

Her fingers pressed against the chest of her gown, as if he had hurt her heart. "How terrible! You must be so worried."

Her concern pushed him to his feet and set them to moving. "I cannot stop thinking of her. She is all I have of Adelaide, my wife. She is so tiny, so innocent. How can I look in her eyes and tell her I failed to do my utmost?"

"You cannot," she said in conviction. "No one who cares for a child can."

He came back to her, knelt on the floor at her feet. The cat leaped away behind the sofa as if he had invaded her space. Perhaps he had. Ivy sat perfectly still, hands folded in her lap.

He took one, feeling the strength of it through his gloves. "Ivy, I have seen the care you give your sisters. You make a house a home. I covet that for Sophia. Marry me, be her mother, save her life. In return, I promise to care for you and your sisters. I will sponsor them, introduce them, provide them with dowries to attract any husband they wish. You will be my marchioness while I live, and I will leave you a home and income in my will. None of you will ever want for anything. Will you help me and Sophia?"

CHAPTER THREE

Ivy and her sisters would never want for anything if she could bring herself to accept his offer. She could not deny the attraction of the thought. Matthew had done well by them, but she remembered the years when her mother had gone hungry so her children could eat. Worse, she remembered the day when Mrs. Bateman had forced them to serve in their own home, threatening and berating them while keeping anything good to herself. Stealing was a sin, but Ivy had crept down to the pantry any number of nights and sliced thin pieces off the ham and roast, the day-old hunks of bread, to keep Daisy and Petunia fed. She'd even baked extra treats and hidden them for her sisters. To know such days were forever behind her—what a gift!

But that lovely vision was wrong. She would still want. She wanted now—to hear him say he loved her, not just that he needed her.

Was that selfish? Always she had put Daisy and Tuny's needs before her own. That's what her mother had done. That's what the Bible required. That's how Matthew lived now. Truly, that was what Lord Kendall was doing. He had no wish for a second wife, but his Sophia needed a mother.

She knew how to be a mother.

She knew what this marriage would mean for her family as well. Daisy fretted so about their place in Society. If Charlotte as the daughter of a viscount could open doors for them, how much more could the regard of a marquess? And dowries! Matthew would do what he could, but this man could give her sisters a future with any man they chose.

Lord Kendall was on one knee, gaze on hers, waiting. Fine lines fanned out from his eyes. It seemed she wasn't the only one wondering about this proposal. Once she'd dreamed of a proposal from the man she loved, of accepting with joy in her heart. Was it right to accept when she felt no joy? Was it wrong to accept for her family's sake?

As if determined to protect her, Fortune stalked out from behind the couch, put her paws on Lord Kendall's knee, and glared up at him, tail swishing.

Ivy leaned back. "Please. Do get up."

He set the cat gently aside and climbed to his feet. Fortune paced back and forth in front of him, tail in the air, back up, ears tight, as if challenging him to combat.

He returned to the chair and sat. "I take it you decline."

His voice was so heavy Ivy hurt for him. Twice in the last month he had come to her aid—once by taking her in secret to see her brother box for the prince and once by helping her find Petunia when her sister had disappeared. He had been a true friend then. He had been honest with her now. She could do no less.

"I am not declining," she told him. As he raised his head, she hurried on. "Neither am I accepting. I understand the honor you have given me, my lord. I never thought to receive a proposal from a gentleman like you. But I had dreamed of a love match. Can you give me no hope of one someday?"

His eyes dipped at the corners. "Alas, Ivy, I cannot. My heart, once given, does not easily give again."

How extraordinary. She had loved her mother, father, and brother. That love had only expanded with the births of Daisy and Tuny. Now it had grown yet again with the addition of Charlotte to their family. Had he focused all emotions on his dead wife?

What would it be like to win such a devotion for herself?

Dangerous thought. He offered her nothing of his love. Yet she knew love could grow. He clearly cared for his daughter. Might he someday come to care for her as well? Was she willing to risk her future on a chance?

"I understand," she murmured, gaze dropping to Fortune. The cat had discovered the tassel on Lord Kendall's boot and had forsaken her military position in front of him to attack it instead. Would that Ivy was distracted so easily.

"Do you at least envision us remaining friends?" she asked her would-be suitor. "Partners in caring for little Sophia?"

"Yes." The answer was swift and heartfelt, as if he clung to any hope she would offer. "Exactly so. You would in all other ways be my lady."

A lady. Lady Kendall. It was more than anyone except Charlotte had ever dreamed for her. She should not wish away such an opportunity.

And yet...

"Tell me about Sophia," she said.

Again, he did not hesitate. "She is as beautiful as her mother and, I fear, as likely to leave us. She cries for hours, and nothing comforts her. She has gained only a few pounds since she was born seven months ago."

That didn't sound good. Daisy had doubled in weight the first seven months. Tuny had gained less, but she too had been missing a mother. Oh, Ivy knew families where babies were put out to nurse, away from the mother that bore them. She had never understood why. Except in cases where the mother was sickly or the home unsafe for a baby, why not keep the precious child close? An unsettling number of babies sent out to nurse died. Small wonder Lord Kendall worried for his daughter.

"And when Sophia is strong and healthy?" Ivy asked. "What do you hope for her?"

The smile he gave her was brighter than any she'd seen. "I'll teach her to ride, to marvel over the constellations, to watch for the changing of the seasons in all their glory. I'll tell her about the Roman antiquities our family has preserved, explain why we must remember our past. I'll gown her in silk, whatever color and style she desires, and the softest wool and velvet. I imagine she will wrap me around her littlest finger."

She likely would. A mother could help prevent him from spoiling the little girl.

And truly, that was what Ivy had loved most growing up—being a mother to Daisy and Tuny. Sometimes when acquaintances learned of her background, they exclaimed over her sacrifice, her nobility. It hadn't felt noble at the time; it still didn't. She loved her family. She'd done what she could to keep them healthy and happy. Charlotte had tried so hard to make her into a Society belle, someone who danced and flirted and exchanged pleasantries over steaming cups of tea. But in her heart, Ivy knew what made her happiest, where she was best suited. A house in the country, far from the stress of the London Season, with a little girl who desperately needed her.

And perhaps, perhaps, the answer to her heart's deepest longing.

She took a breath. "Then I will marry you, my lord, and be Sophia's mother."

She'd agreed. Joy pushed Kendall to his feet, but guilt kept him from reaching for Ivy. He should not feel such delight in taking a second wife. He was marrying for Sophia's safe, after all, not his own.

"Thank you," he told Ivy. "I will petition the Archbishop of Canterbury for a special license today. We can be married and back in Surrey within the week."

Her face fell even as she came to stand beside him. "So soon? Matthew and Charlotte won't be back from their honeymoon by then. I would not want to marry without them."

Again, he felt like a churl. He was giving her a considerable amount, financially and socially, but he could not shake the feeling that he was the one most benefitting. "Understood, but every day away from Sophia is one day more that she lacks the comfort she needs. I am told she cries every time I leave."

She bit her lower lip, which was a warm rosy color that reminded him of the deep pink orchids his mother had planted in the conservatory. He forced himself to gaze into her eyes instead. They were equally warm, inviting him closer.

He stayed where he was.

"Perhaps," she allowed, "since it isn't a love match, we can marry without my brother and Charlotte. But I would like Daisy, Petunia, and Miss Thorn to attend."

"Of course," he agreed, relief relaxing shoulders he hadn't realized were so tense. "And thank you, Ivy. You are more understanding than I have any right to expect. Will St. George's Hanover Square do?"

"Yes. Let me know the day and time once you're spoken with the vicar."

"I will." Despite the feelings tugging at him, he reached out and took her hand. "I will be a considerate husband. I promise."

"And I will do my best to be a good mother to Sophia," she vowed.

He squeezed her hand and released her. "I'll send word soon." He moved toward the door, though something urged him to stay.

A grey flash passed him on the stairs. He nearly pulled up before he realized it was Fortune. It wasn't the first time the cat had followed him to the door. Now she scampered under the hall table and peered out at him.

"Congratulations, my lord," the butler intoned, offering him his high-crowned hat and walking stick.

What, had the fellow been listening at the door? He tried to imagine that tall, regal frame bent over a keyhole.

"Thank you," he said, accepting his belongings. As he slipped his hat onto his head, Fortune darted out from under the table and attacked his tassel.

The butler bent to retrieve her. She stared at Kendall accusingly, as if she knew his thoughts were not those of a besotted bridegroom. He let himself out.

The feelings persisted as he obtained the special license and booked the chapel for eight Thursday morning. When he'd married Adelaide, there had been weeks of preparation—a new suit for him, a full trousseau for her. Friends and family had held parties and balls in their honor. They'd ordered vase upon vase of flowers to decorate her parents' chapel, where they had celebrated the marriage surrounded by all who loved them.

Perhaps he should have waited for Sir Matthew to return. Yet, truth be told, he was a little concerned Ivy's brother might take exception to the match. How would he react? He was a former pugilist. Kendall had seen him fight. He would not want to face those fists. Better to present the happy bride, *fait accompli*.

Besides his main reason for hurrying her wasn't her brother or even Sophia. If they wed quickly, he would not have the opportunity to change his mind.

He could, however, arrange for flowers. He wrote to his land steward, explained the situation, asked him to alert the staff at the house to expect them Thursday evening. The orchids, roses, and gardenias began arriving Wednesday afternoon, and Kendall's town staff placed them in silver vases and moved them into the chapel before the bride and her party arrived.

Even with all his efforts, he very nearly did change his mind as Ivy and her sisters walked up the aisle to meet him. When he'd wed Adelaide, his brother Weston had stood up with him, proud in the scarlet of his military uniform, newly won. Now Wes was away on the Peninsula, as were many of the men Kendall had called friend at Eton. He could think of no one he wanted at his side. He was only glad Miss Thorn had brought her betrothed, the solicitor Mr. Julian Mayes with her, so that they had the required two witnesses of mature age. The fellow smiled politely as he stood off to one side, hair nearly as red-gold as the candlesticks on the altar.

Kendall and Ivy stood before the vicar. On one side, Daisy and Petunia held bouquets of cream-colored gardenias, their dusky stems wrapped in yellow satin ribbon. Adelaide had married in satin. Ivy wore white muslin, a simple gown with a few ruffles around the softly arched neck and at the cuffs and hem. He'd given her no time to commission a new gown. A fine husband he was starting out to be.

He took her hand as directed, spoke the vows he'd never thought to say again. He wasn't sure who was paler, him or Ivy. The vicar regarded them with a frown, as if wondering why they had decided to marry in the first place. Kendall straightened, put on his best smile.

"Wilt thou love her, comfort her, honor and keep her, in sickness and in health, and, forsaking all other, keep thee only unto her, so long as ye both shall live?"

It was a simple response. All he had to say was *I will.* Yet the words froze on his tongue. Forsaking all other, even Adelaide?

As if she knew his conflict, Ivy squeezed his hand, smile encouraging. Her kindness banished the guilt. She understood. She too entered the marriage with hopes of benefiting those she loved.

"I will," he said.

The ceremony proceeded through the reading of the

psalms, the short sermon. Then the vicar smiled and nodded to those gathered. "May I present Lord and Lady Kendall?"

Miss Thorn and Mr. Mayes stepped forward to shake their hands. Petunia beamed at him. Daisy threw her arms about him and gave him a hug.

"Now I have a brother who's a knight and a brother who's a marquess," she told him.

He smiled at her as she disengaged and caught a movement from the corner of his eye. A shadow slipped across the back of the church, a man heading for the door. Kendall saw only the back of him as he exited, narrow shoulders, shabby coat, tweed cap.

Why had he been attending their wedding unannounced, and why had he left without coming forward to congratulate them?

CHAPTER FOUR

On Julian's arm, Meredith followed Ivy and Lord Kendall down the aisle for the door of St. George's.

"Thinking about our vows?" Julian murmured in her ear.

Her long-time beau had only recently proposed to her, for all she'd asked him to marry her when they were young. Meredith had never been happier than when she'd accepted him. The banns were even now being read, and they planned to wed at the home of her former client and friend, Jane, Duchess of Wey, in August.

"Actually, I'm more concerned about Ivy's vows," she told Julian as they reached the massive wood door. "Some nervousness on the part of the bride is to be expected, but her groom looked as if he was on the way to a hanging—his own."

"Lord Kendall is a good sort," Julian assured her. "Sir Alexander managed his father's affairs, and his."

The mention of Julian's mentor sent a chill through her. "Just as well Sir Alexander was off in America for the last few months, negotiating for the King. I do not like to think what he'd say about this match. Or ours."

Julian brought her hand to his lips as they stepped out into the sunlit pavement before the stone church. "You have no need for concern, Meredith. Nothing he could say would diminish my regard for you."

She believed that. She and Julian loved each other, had been through much before finding their way back to each other. But Sir Alexander Prentice had helped orchestrate the worst moments of her life. He would likely have stopped at nothing to prevent her from marrying the man he had helped groom as a solicitor. If she never saw the fellow again, it would be too soon.

She was married. The thought still seemed foreign as Ivy stood before Matthew's house off Covent Garden, preparing to leave for her new life. She wiggled her shoulders in the green redingote she wore over her soft blue wool travel gown. She didn't feel any different, for all she'd just pledged her life to another. Her straw bonnet crackled as she turned her head to glance at Lord Kendall, as he waited for her trunks to be loaded on his travel coach. It was a wonder the massive beast fit into the little lane that had been her home in London for the last few years.

"Do you have dogs?" Petunia asked Lord Kendall from the pavement beside them.

Daisy, standing next to her with Miss Thorn, snorted. "All lords have hounds, silly."

"Actually, I've never been much for riding to hounds," Lord Kendall said. "It always felt terribly unfair to the fox."

Ivy couldn't help her smile at that.

"Cats, then?" Tuny pressed as Daisy rolled her eyes.

"Perhaps in the barns," he allowed.

Tuny frowned as if disappointed in him. "A chicken or two?"

"Possibly."

"What are their names?" Petunia demanded before Ivy could edge her into another line of conversation. "May I have one of the chicks?"

"You may not," Ivy managed to put in. "There's little room for Rufus as it is. I don't want to know where you'd keep a chicken."

Petunia's look turned mutinous. A shame Matthew was gone. Ivy would have liked to warn him about this new fascination. Chickens off Covent Garden. What would the neighbors say?

Lord Kendall gave her sister a commiserating smile beneath his neat mustache. "Perhaps you could come visit this summer. We could examine the chickens together."

Tuny nodded, grin turning up.

"If you're hosting a house party," Daisy put in, moving closer with a swish of her muslin skirts, "I don't see why we must bring the infantry."

Tuny bristled. Ivy stepped in from long habit. "Lord Kendall is not hosting a house party. I have many duties to learn before I'm comfortable with guests. But family is always welcome."

He eyed her, and she took a breath. Who was she to make such a pronouncement? She had no right to decide who was and wasn't invited. But he had asked her to join her life to his. He had to know her family was part of that bargain.

"I look forward to seeing all of the Batemans," he said, and Ivy nodded, smile returning.

But it was impossible to keep smiling as she took her farewells. She could remember a time before Daisy and Petunia were born, but they could not remember a time before her. Would they miss her as much as she'd miss them?

Tuny seemed to think so. She hugged Ivy hard. "I will think about you every day," she promised. "Write me letters. I'll write back."

"You better," Ivy teased, blinking back tears. "Daisy won't."

"When you host your house party," Daisy said after

NEVER MARRY A MARQUESS   39

giving her a quick hug, "be sure to invite Sir William. Oh, and Chas Prestwick. I hear he's a lot of fun."

"We won't be hosting a house party," Ivy insisted. "Not until Christmas at the earliest."

Daisy frowned. "Well, what good is a sister who's a marchioness if you never get to see her?"

Ivy leaned closer. "You should have thought of that before you locked me in the library."

Daisy laughed.

Ivy squeezed her hand as she straightened. "Be nice to Tuny. Tell Matthew I left a note in his study. It explains everything."

Daisy's smile snuffed out. "Everything?"

"Ready to go, my lord," the coachman called.

Tuny and Daisy stepped back, her littlest sister crying openly. Ivy's heart twisted inside her.

No. She must not worry about them. They were old enough to take care of themselves. She'd seen to that. If anything more was needed, Charlotte was clever. She'd figure it out. Another little girl needed Ivy more.

Miss Thorn, who had remained back as if determined not to intrude, now came forward. "I expect to hear only good things in the future, my lord."

Lord Kendall touched his top hat. "I will endeavor to make it so, Miss Thorn." He dropped his arm to offer it to Ivy. "Shall we?"

Ivy swallowed, but she put her hand on his arm, and he helped her up into the coach.

Her family had never owned a carriage, but she'd ridden in hired coaches as well as Charlotte's family carriage. They had been comfortable, but tight, built for town driving. The Marquess of Kendall's travel coach was much wider, with richly paneled walls and seats of deep blue velvet more padded than most armchairs. The equipage moved so sleekly that she scarcely felt the cobblestones as the coachman angled them into the traffic surrounding

Covent Garden.

It was hard to look out the window with her bonnet. Ivy removed it and set it in her lap, smiling at the green grosgrain ribbons Daisy had used to trim it. No, it was probably best not to think about her family right then, or she'd be tempted to throw herself out of the coach. She chanced a glance at her husband—her husband!—who had seated himself across from her for all there was plenty of room beside her. His smile remained polite, his posture upright. He still wore his hat. Did he too want to jump out and run back to a time when things were less complicated?

"We should reach Hampton before dinner," he told her.

"Will we stop to eat?" Ivy asked. Not that her stomach would allow it. It seemed to have wrapped itself into a tight little ball inside her.

"If you'd like. We will stop to change horses in any event. We keep a set there for just such occasions."

He had so many horses he would leave them about the countryside. *What did you expect, Ivy? He's a marquess.*

"Let's see how we feel," she temporized.

He inclined his head, then arched his back ever the slightest, as if trying to make himself more comfortable. Daisy claimed riding with her back to their destination for any distance made her bilious. Would his position affect him the same way?

"You may sit beside me," Ivy said, scooting closer to the paneled wall.

With a smile, he swung himself across, and even though a foot of space lay between them now, the bench felt unaccountably smaller.

"Have you been to Surrey before?" he asked.

Ivy shook her head. "We had never been out of Birmingham before Matthew brought us down to London, and we didn't go through Surrey. Do you like it there?"

He stretched out his legs on the polished wood floor. "Very much so. My estate is on a slight hill, bounded by rivers lined with trees. You can see for miles."

She could not imagine that. Covent Garden and Hyde Park were the largest areas she'd ever visited, and even there one could not see beyond a few yards in most places. The piazza at Covent Garden was too full of people. Many parts of the park were too full of trees.

"And the house, my lord?" she asked.

She applauded herself for making polite conversation. That's what Charlotte said one was to do with a gentleman. Still, he turned his head and eyed her as if she'd said something extraordinary. Her cheeks started heating.

"Since we are married," he said, "we can surely dispense with my lord and my lady."

So that was the reason he was looking at her so oddly. Ivy dropped her gaze to the bonnet in her lap. "You never gave me leave to use your first name."

"How remiss of me. My name is Stephen, but I've never gone by that. Since coming into the title, I prefer Kendall."

It was not as intimate, but then, they had no intention of being intimate. "If it pleases you, Kendall."

"It pleases me a great deal. Allow me to say again how much I appreciate your willingness to join me in this effort, Ivy."

An effort. Not a marriage. Not the meeting of minds and hearts. She'd known that. Why did the thought prick at her, as if she'd misjudged the placement of her needle while hemming?

"We are family now," she said, raising her head to meet his gaze. "Family helps one another."

"Well said," he replied.

Silence reigned, at least in the interior of the mighty coach. Outside, the crowded streets of London had given way to the green of field and garden, the elegance of country estates. Would her new home look so stately? Would she find her footing there?

"Your family is welcome to visit anytime," he ventured.

Polite conversation again. She should contribute. Ivy composed her face and her thoughts. "You mentioned a brother. Will he visit too?"

"Not for a while," he admitted, hands on his knees. "We are ten months apart and were close growing up, but he chose a military career. He's an officer in the Twelfth Dragoons."

An impressive regiment. She'd read about them in the paper. They were even now fighting on the Peninsula. "You must be proud."

His mustache twitched. "Weston is proud. I worry more for him. He was always the brasher of the two of us."

"Like Daisy," she mused. "I often wonder what Mother would have thought of us now."

He sighed. "Unfortunately, neither of us remembers our mother, only the stories we were told of her."

Sadness stole over her. "Daisy and Petunia don't remember our mother either."

"But you remember?"

Ivy smiled. "Yes. Her hair was like mine, and she generally wore it up. She had the softest smile, like a brush of a butterfly's wing."

He nodded. "You favor her, I think."

He could not know the praise he'd given her. "Oh, but I hope so. My mother taught me how to love, in any circumstance. That is a rare gift."

Now he examined his hands. "I envy you. My father did his best, but he had no idea how to raise us. He had never been close to his own father. Such matters were left to nursemaids, nannies, tutors. I want more for Sophia."

Once again she felt the pain radiating from him, like heat from an oven. Ivy lay her hand over his. "We will give her more."

He met her gaze, the lines of his face softening. Something simmered in the brown, welcoming her. Was it any more real than her tenuous hopes?

Her eyes were brown, a lighter shade than his, and he had never noticed how thick her lashes were, like strands of gold against her cheeks. They fluttered now, and her skin turned pink, as if she recognized his attention.

He shifted, and her hand fell to the velvet.

"You asked about the house earlier," he said. Yes, that was the ticket. The weather, the estate. Anyone might have commented on them. There was nothing overly familiar about the topics. And he could look away without diving into her gaze.

"Yes," Ivy said. She sat taller, as if gathering herself as well. "What's it like? What do you love about it?"

There was that word, the word that could not be spoken between them. But it was perfectly fine to share what he admired about his home. In fact, it was remarkably easy.

"I think I appreciate the history of it most," he told her. "The estate has been in my family for seven generations, but the first evidence we have found of a settlement dates back to Roman times."

"Romans." She seized on the word. "I've read about them. They were a mighty army that had swept across the Continent, across even England. Did they build a fortress on your lands?"

He removed his hat and tossed it across to the empty seat. "Not a fortress. We believe the area to have been used as a clay works."

Her eyes sparkled. "Clay works? As in trade? I thought marquesses were supposed to be above such things."

"We never practiced the trade," he said with an answering smile. "We merely protected the remains of it. The first Marquess of Kendall conducted the initial investigation. My great-grandfather took it one step further, enclosing the ruins in an Italian villa, Villa Romanesque."

Her brows went up. "An Italian villa, in Surrey?"

He imagined the owners of the neighboring estates had initially reacted the same way. "There are others—Marble Hill House, Nympton. In any event, my father and I have worked to ensure the remains are protected for future generations."

She licked her lips, and now his gaze latched onto the rosy pink, as soft looking as petals. "Remains. Dead bodies?"

He jerked his gaze away. "No, no. No bodies. Whoever left this establishment moved on, as we found few belongings. The most marvelous piece is a mosaic pavement. I'll show you when we reach the house."

She nodded eagerly. "I would greatly enjoy seeing that."

Perhaps as much as he would enjoy showing her. His passion, Adelaide had teased him. The only thing capable of taking him from her side for long. Until she had left his side forever.

Ivy was watching him expectantly. Had she asked him a question?

"Sorry," he said. "Woolgathering."

She titled her head to one side. "And what marquess gathers wool with the farmers?"

How easily she made him smile. "What else can I tell you?"

"An Italian villa sounds like a cozy home. How many rooms are there, all told?"

He frowned, skimming over the plans of the house in his mind. "Forty to fifty, I suppose, around the center plaza."

She stared at him. "Forty to fifty?"

"Yes, nothing too ungainly. I know some of the larger country houses boast more than two hundred rooms, but I never saw the need for anything larger. I hope you don't mind."

She visibly swallowed. "No, I don't mind. It sounds quite large to me. I would not want to clean so many rooms."

Her voice had a breathless sound to it, as if she feared he might set her to such a task.

He waved a hand. "I leave the cleaning and maintenance to Mrs. Sheppard, our housekeeper. Though I imagine she will want your direction. You are the marchioness."

All color fled. "Yes, I suppose I am."

And she did not look the least bit happy about it.

CHAPTER FIVE

Villa Romanesque. What a name for an English estate. Ivy could only stare out the window in trepidation as the carriage rolled up a gently sweeping drive to the front of the house. The summer sun, low in the sky, made the white stone gleam like a pearl, yet every angle of corner and roof was precise, a massive block on each side. Even the gardens across the gravel drive from the front door were laid out in squares and triangles, the thick green hedges cropped low and perfectly flat, so that not one leaf was out of line. She had never seen nature so controlled.

Then again, she hadn't seen much of nature, having been raised in the city. How amazing to see fields of rippling grain stretching in every direction until they lapped against the wall of trees to the east and west. Those must mark the rivers he'd mentioned, making their way to the mighty Thames.

And the servants! As the coach drew to a stop, Kendall's staff came running from the stables to one side, spilled out of the three-story house. Groomsmen took charge of the horses; footmen hoisted off the trunks. Men in black tailcoats and women in grey gowns covered by simple white aprons lined the path from the coach to the wide arched front door.

Kendall climbed down, turned, and offered her his hand. "Welcome home, Ivy."

She wanted to stay in her seat, beg the coachman to return her to London. This wasn't a home; it was far too grand.

And this marriage was a mistake. If she hadn't fit into London Society, how could she possibly fit in here? The housekeeper would take one look at her and send her to the servants quarters, if she was even good enough to serve there. She fumbled to put her bonnet back on with the insane idea that it might make her look more presentable.

As if he saw her fear, Kendall leaned into the coach. "You are Lady Kendall now. This is your staff. You dance to no one's tune."

Ivy stilled. How amazing. All her life, she'd done what needed to be done. She loved Daisy and Tuny, had been proud to keep Matthew's house. But always, someone else had made the decisions—her father, Mrs. Bateman, Matthew, even Charlotte and Miss Thorn.

Here, at least some of the decisions would be hers. She could not doubt him. That face was too solemn, too sure.

She put her hand on his and stepped down from the coach.

He tucked her hand in his arm and smiled as he turned toward the waiting staff. At the end of the line, the door stood open as if to welcome her. The rounded pediment over the door was carved with the face of an elderly man, hair long and eyes bulging. He might have been beaming approval.

Or laughing that she thought she had any place here.

A woman came forward to greet them. She was past middle-age, grey threading the sleek black tresses confined in a bun at the top of her head. Cool blue eyes regarded Ivy steadily from a face smooth of line, blemish, or emotion.

"Lady Kendall," the marquess said, "allow me to introduce Mrs. Sheppard, our housekeeper."

The housekeeper curtsied, and Ivy had to stop herself from returning the gesture.

"Lady Kendall is new to Surrey," he explained. "I expect you will explain our ways of doing things."

Mrs. Sheppard inclined her head, and Ivy smiled her appreciation.

"However," Kendall continued, "if she has a different approach, I expect you to listen and obey."

Mrs. Sheppard blinked. Ivy stared at Kendall. Did he understand the power he'd just conferred on her?

"Of course, my lord," the housekeeper said, breaking the stunned silence. She had a precise way of speaking, as if making sure each vowel and consonant had its proper time and place. "And I will be sure to bring the matter to you for approval."

Kendall wouldn't give her even that little concession. "No need. I trust Lady Kendall in all things. Now, would you be so good as to introduce the staff?"

The only sign of the housekeeper's shock at his statement was a quirk of her black brows, but she turned to lead them up the walk, pausing every few steps to comment on the staff member standing on either side.

Ivy did her best to remember the name and positions, but by the fifth set of them, her brain balked. It didn't help that there were more than one of many positions (how many upstairs maids did a house need?) and similar or duplicate names. Martha the elder was a downstairs maid while Martha the younger worked in the laundry in an outbuilding behind the house, and neither would have been pleased to be confused with the other. Parkins was a groom, but Perkins was an underfootman, and she knew enough about the positions to understand one worked outside and the other in. A shame there wasn't some book listing who was who as there was for the aristocracy— *Debrett's Peerage of the Servants of Villa Romanesque.*

One thing they all shared was their tension. Every body was tight, every gaze pinched with worry. Did they doubt Ivy knew how to manage them? She certainly did.

As they reached the door, Ivy drew in a breath of relief. But the housekeeper wasn't finished yet.

"Will we need to add your maid to the staff, your ladyship?" she asked, hands clasped before her grey gown. "Make other changes in positions?"

Someone behind her muttered a prayer. Glancing back, Ivy saw every gaze on her. Martha the elder was visibly trembling. Parkins, no, no, Perkins was white. Small wonder they were so tense. They thought the new mistress of the house might want her own staff close. They were afraid she'd toss them out.

Ivy gave them an encouraging smile before turning to the housekeeper. She raised her voice just the slightest, so even Martha the younger at the edge of the drive would hear.

"My sisters had need of our maid, so I could not bring her with me," Ivy explained. "And Lord Kendall has given me nothing but praise for his staff. I could not imagine replacing a single one."

Air wafted past her, as if all thirty-seven staff members— she'd counted at least—had exhaled at the same time.

"Very good, your ladyship," Mrs. Sheppard said, stern lips hinting of a smile at last. "There are two staff missing, but you'll meet them shortly. Nurse Wilman and Becky Bradley have charge of the nursery."

Kendall took her elbow. "Perhaps we should go there now."

If the housekeeper heard the concern in his voice, she did not acknowledge it. She stepped aside, and the head footman, Travis, opened the door to admit Kendall and Ivy.

My, but Kendall's great-grandfather had favored marble. White stone veined in silver circled the columns holding up the high ceiling of the entry hall. White marble tile spaced with black covered the expanse of floor. White marble flanked the hearth that warmed the space and crowned the tread of the stairs rising to the next story.

Stairs placed in a stairway that turned at precise angles, of course.

Travis remained with Mrs. Sheppard to deal with the staff, and Kendall and Ivy took the stairs. Their footsteps echoed as they climbed, but another sound rose louder.

A baby. Crying.

The sound raged with pain, frustration. It demanded a response. Each breath urged Ivy closer, propelled her steps, until she was the one leading Kendall. She did not have to ask the way. The cry drew her to the top story and a closed door along a plastered corridor.

Kendall caught up with her before she could seize the latch. "Allow me. We wouldn't want to startle her." He opened the door slowly, as if expecting a lion to leap out at them.

The curtains had been drawn against the sun; only a glow appeared over the top and around the sides. The light came predominantly from a fire that burned much too hot for a summer's day. Sitting in an oak rocker beside it, a heavyset elderly woman calmly worked at a bit of lace, pleated cap covering her hair. A younger woman, not much older than Daisy, flitted here and there as if she didn't know what to do next.

Ivy knew. That crib against the far wall. The cries came from the depths. She started forward, and Kendall touched her arm. She looked at him askance. Even in the dim light, she could see that he had paled.

"A moment," he said.

A moment? Why did he wait? Didn't those ragged cries touch his heart? She could barely force herself to stand calmly.

And why were neither of the nursery staff moving to help the baby? Both had stopped what they were doing when Ivy and Kendall had entered. Now the girl bobbed a curtsey, and the older woman climbed to her feet and did the same.

"Lady Kendall," her husband continued, though he had to raise his voice over the wails. "May I present the nursery staff?"

Ivy couldn't take it any longer. "No," she told him. "Someone needs to see to poor Sophia. Now."

Her words fired another arrow into his heart. Every time he called her Lady Kendall, a voice in his head labeled him a traitor. There was only one Lady Kendall, and she resided in the graveyard at the back of the church. Yet if his staff were to respect Ivy, he must lead the way.

"Nurse Wilman, if you would be so kind," he said.

Nurse Wilman drew herself up, wrinkled face determined. "Babies will only cry all the more if they are held every time they squall. Anyone who has raised children knows that."

"Nonsense," Ivy said, breaking away from him and heading for the crib. "I've raised two, and my sisters never cried for attention."

She was bending over the crib before Kendall could reach her side. One look at his daughter only tightened the knot in his chest. Those wide blue eyes that so often swam with tears, the black curls, the soft skin—she was Adelaide in miniature. At the sight of him peering over the carved railings, she scrunched up her reddened face and howled, thrashing about under the cover of the blankets.

"There, now." Ivy reached in and picked her up, then began unfurling the thick flannel. "Were you too confined, my sweet girl?"

He stiffened, every part of him crying out to take his daughter from her. Yet he'd married Ivy for this purpose. He had told his staff he trusted her with all household decisions. He must trust her with Sophia as well.

"My lord, I protest," Nurse Wilman said, huffing up to them. "I raised your father, you and your brother, and your two cousins as well. You cannot replace me with this untried stranger."

Ivy paid her not the least attention, rocking Sophia and cooing to her. Were his daughter's cries slowing? He'd heard them so often he could no longer tell.

"And Becky has been the best of the lot," his nurse continued. "She's a bit flighty, but she does just what I say."

As if determined to keep her distance, the brown-haired nursemaid took another step back, bumping into the wall.

"I'm glad to hear Becky is helpful," Ivy said, smoothing Sophia's hair back from her face. "Becky, open the curtains and a window."

Nurse Wilman yelped. "Do nothing of the kind. The light hurts Lady Sophia's eyes."

Did it? Doctor Penrose had never mentioned she had a weakness in her vision. Kendall kept his chin up to keep from searching her gaze.

Sophia rubbed her face against Ivy's chest, plucked at her gown. But now he was certain. Her crying was softer, punctuated by sniffs.

"The light may indeed sting, if she's been kept in the dark for days," Ivy allowed. "But she will grow accustomed to it. And it is entirely too hot in here."

He couldn't argue there. He wanted to throw off his coat and roll up his shirtsleeves.

Nurse Wilman thought otherwise. "Babies need warmth and dark," she protested.

"The only thing that grows in warmth and dark is rot," Ivy countered. "Becky, open the window."

Becky swayed from foot to foot, gaze darting from one woman to another, then appealing to Kendall for aid. Though he knew he had to allow Ivy to fight this fight, he inclined his head just the slightest. Becky edged toward the window.

"Doctor Penrose won't like it," Nurse Wilman threatened. "He left strict orders."

"I would like to see them," Ivy said, bouncing Sophia up and down in her arms.

The nurse glared at her. "He told me personally. I'm the head of this nursery."

The two women locked gazes. In the silence, he heard a coal settle in the grate.

The silence.

Panic made him seize Sophia at last, pulling her out of Ivy's grip and gazing into her little face. Was she having a fit? Had she died?

In the dim light, his daughter blinked big blue eyes, then widened her mouth. He readied himself for the roar.

Instead, she smiled at him.

Smiled. For the first time. He wanted to shout, he wanted to dance, he wanted to throw up his hands in praise to a merciful God. Instead, he carefully remanded his precious daughter back into Ivy's arms.

"Becky," he said, "do whatever Lady Kendall tells you to do. Nurse Wilman, I expect you to do the same, without complaint or hesitation, or I will return you to a well-earned retirement."

The nurse gasped and clutched her generous chest, but the maid rushed to the south-facing windows and yanked open the curtains to let sunlight flood the room. His daughter blinked again. He glanced up to see Ivy's smile.

"Thank you, Kendall," she said.

"No," Kendall said, gaze returning to his beautiful daughter. "Thank you. Thank you with all my heart."

CHAPTER SIX

That was the first time Ivy had caught him in a lie. As the nurse continued to bluster, Ivy shook her head. Kendall's relief at the smile on his beautiful daughter's face was evident by his look of awe, but he couldn't thank Ivy with all his heart. His heart wasn't involved in their partnership.

Sophia began to fuss again, and he stiffened. Ivy set about rocking her in her arms. She was so tiny. Her little hands would barely wrap around one of his fingers. Tuny had been small, but not like this. Ivy just wanted to sit in the rocker and hold the baby until they both found some peace. But the wiser course was to determine the cause of the crying.

"Has she been changed recently?" Ivy interrupted the nurse's tirade.

Kendall shifted on his feet as if none too comfortable with the question. Nurse Wilman snapped her mouth shut and adjusted her skirts as if trying to determine a polite way to respond to the interloper in her domain.

"Not an hour ago, your ladyship," Becky put in from the safety of the far wall.

So, not that, then. Indeed, she felt no undue warmth against her arm. "When was the last time she ate?"

Kendall answered that question. "Doctor Penrose advised a strict schedule, to help her gain weight."

Nurse Wilman raised her head. "Gruel every four hours, day and night."

How odd. Their mother had breastfed Daisy until she turned one but had begun weaning her at six months onto greater sustenance. They hadn't been able to afford a live-in wet-nurse for Tuny, and Ivy hadn't been willing to place her out, so her little sister had had to go on gruel when their mother had died. Ivy still remembered boiling and straining the liquid into the little boat-shaped bottles. She'd had to feed Tuny nearly as frequently as the nurse was feeding Sophia at first. But not at seven months.

"No solid food?" she pressed.

"She's far too sickly to abide solids," the nurse declared.

Perhaps. But perhaps one of the reasons she was sickly was because she needed more than weak gruel. "And she cries like this often?"

"Too often," Kendall murmured, brow furrowing as if he felt his daughter's pain.

"She had the colic at first," Nurse Wilman explained, widening her stance. "Babies with colic cry. You just have to get through it."

She'd been blessed that neither Tuny nor Daisy had been struck with colic, but she'd talked to mothers near them in Birmingham who had lived through the ordeal. Still, most babies had outgrown the cruel stomach pains by now.

She studied the baby in her arms. Lady Sophia studied her back, blue eyes unblinking. What was going through that little mind? As Ivy watched, the baby grimaced, and one hand moved up to rub at her jaw. Ivy peered closer.

"And there's your culprit at the moment," she said, straightening. "She's teething."

"What?" Kendall bent over the child in her arms, sable hair brushing her cheek. She caught the scent of something spicy, like the sandalwood fan her mother had owned. Was that his cologne? She wanted to breathe in deep.

"I don't see it," he said, scanning his daughter's face.

Sophia offered him a watery smile.

Ivy gathered her thoughts and balanced the baby in one arm so she could thumb back Sophia's lower lip with her free hand.

"A tooth!" Kendall grinned at Ivy as if they'd just discovered gold in the well.

"And another on the way, I expect," Ivy said, warm in his regard. "Perhaps we could dip a rag in cold water for her to chew on. That should help with the ache."

"A rag? A rag!" Nurse Wilman sputtered. "Lady Sophia will not chew on some rag."

Kendall straightened with a frown. Did he too feel the suggestion too lowly for the daughter of a marquess? Well, princess or pauper, babies had the same needs.

"Make it silk if you prefer," Ivy said, irritation building. "But she won't stop crying if you do nothing."

"Laudanum," the nurse said with a nod. "A dose would put her right out."

Kendall turned white.

Ivy thought she must be turning red. Certainly heat flushed up her at the mention of the drug that had sent more than one woman into oblivion. She didn't think it was the temperature of the room. She was angry. She was rarely angry. That wasn't her nature. But something fierce wrapped around her now. Was this how Matthew had felt when Mrs. Bateman had made his sisters' lives so difficult?

She couldn't react the way he used to react. She would not raise her fist. She seldom raised her voice. But she would do so now for little Sophia.

She moved away from the nurse. "You will not use the essence of opium on Lady Sophia. Not today. Not ever."

Perhaps she had some of Matthew's presence after all, for Becky pressed herself against the wall, and Nurse Wilman visibly gulped.

Ivy looked to Kendall, who was eyeing her as if wondering whether she'd turn on him too. "My lord, perhaps you and

Nurse Wilman could step into the other room and discuss her retirement, as you suggested."

The woman narrowed her eyes at Ivy. "I know when I'm not wanted. But Lady Kendall trusted me to take care of her daughter. She wouldn't much appreciate you stepping into her place."

Kendall stiffened, as if every muscle in his body had tightened. Very likely Sophia's mother would be aghast that the daughter of a millworker thought she knew anything about raising the daughter of a marquess. But Ivy refused to back down. Kendall had married her to care for Sophia. Drugging a baby and then refusing comfort was no way to raise a child, aristocrat or commoner. She'd stake her life on it.

"Perhaps I might be of assistance." Mrs. Sheppard moved into the nursery, color nearly as high as the baby's had been. "If I might have a word, my lord, my lady. I'm sure Becky can watch over Lady Sophia for a moment."

Ivy wasn't nearly so sure. Neither was Becky, for she was shrinking in on herself as if she hoped to blend into the pale blue wallpaper.

"Sophia stays with me," Ivy said, and no one argued with her as she carried the baby out into the corridor with Kendall and the housekeeper. Someone shut the door behind her.

"I take it Nurse Wilman did not live up to your expectations, Lady Kendall," the housekeeper said, faint admonishment in her careful voice. "She has given good service, for decades."

"Lady Kendall also has experience," Kendall said, tone grave and implacable.

She would not hide behind him. "Nurse Wilman may have the greater experience, but she is mistaken about how to deal with Lady Sophia."

"Indeed," the housekeeper said, and the word committed to nothing. "And what would you advise doing differently?"

It was a challenge, though one laid down with a velvet glove. Ivy did not hesitate to accept it. "Give her light and air for one. Play with her. Offer her something to stimulate her intellect, encourage her to use her hands and legs. Start her on solid food—pureed at first—vegetables, then grains, then fruits. And I insist that if she starts crying, some effort must be made to determine why and rectify the matter."

She could not remember speaking so forcefully. Kendall certainly had never heard her speak this way. He was regarding her with a slight frown, but at her attitude or her suggestions, she wasn't sure.

"A sensible plan," Mrs. Sheppard said. "Do you concur, my lord?"

He'd said he wouldn't second-guess Ivy, but this was his child. Would he back her up against the woman who had helped raise him?

Kendall's brow cleared. "My direction stands, Mrs. Sheppard. You have no need to appeal to me if Lady Kendall wishes to change things. I have complete faith in her. And I am willing to try anything that might help Sophia."

"Then you no longer wish to keep Nurse Wilman in your employ?" the housekeeper asked.

He glanced at the closed door of the nursery. "I remember the lady fondly. I'm sure Wes does as well. But perhaps it is time she retired."

Ivy wanted to hug him, but she snuggled Sophia closer instead. The baby sighed happily.

"I will make arrangements," Mrs. Sheppard said. "Is Becky to be let go as well?"

Kendall looked to Ivy.

"Becky may stay," Ivy said. "But she must heed my advice. And there are other arrangements that may need to be made." She turned to Kendall. "Where am I to sleep, my lord?"

His frown returned, as if he had not considered the matter.

"Lady Kendall's apartments are on the second story," Mrs. Sheppard put in helpfully.

"Not there," he said.

She could not argue with the swift response. She had no interest in usurping his wife's place any more than necessary. "Certainly not there. Is there a spot near it where you can move the nursery?"

Mrs. Sheppard's brows shot up. "Move the nursery?"

"Yes," Ivy said, arms rocking the baby. "I don't intend to be parted from Lady Sophia until we are all assured of her wellbeing."

Mrs. Sheppard looked to Kendall. Of course she would, despite his requests to the contrary. He had made all the decisions regarding the estate since he had ascended to the title on his father's death two years ago. He'd been trained to the role since birth. He knew the traditions, the protocols. A husband, newly married, would be expected to want his bride close, with no impediment like a crying baby between them. But he and Ivy had a different arrangement.

"My mother's and brother's rooms," he said. "They are on the same floor as mine, but there is a connecting door between the two. Prepare one for Ivy and the other for Sophia."

Mrs. Sheppard inclined her head. "At once, my lord. Let me speak to the staff about the matter, and then I will address the issue of Nurse Wilman. Would you like to see the rooms, Lady Kendall, to ensure they are adequate?"

"I'll show her," Kendall said, and the housekeeper went about her business, grey skirts flapping in her haste.

"I've caused her more work," Ivy said sadly, watching her head down the stairs.

"All part of her job," Kendall said. "And thank you for understanding about Adelaide's rooms. I haven't changed them since she died." His throat tightened, and he coughed to clear it. Safe in Ivy's arms, Sophia regarded him solemnly.

"Of course, my lord," Ivy murmured.

"This way," he said with a wave toward the stairs, and it wasn't until the third step that he realized she had called him my lord again.

He glanced over to where she descended beside him, her gaze veering from the marble treads before her to the baby in her arms. How different she was from Sophia. His daughter was dark-haired, pale-skinned, tiny. Ivy was blond, creamy complexioned, and sturdy. She caught him looking and offered him a smile. The nursery wasn't the only room that felt brighter by her presence.

"I believe an apology is in order," he said as they reached the second story and he turned to the left on the carpeted corridor. "To you and to Sophia. Nurse Wilman raised me and my brother until we were breached. I had no reason to doubt Adelaide's choice when she invited Wilman back from retirement for Sophia."

"Sophia's struggles likely made Nurse Wilman try different tactics than she used on you or your brother," Ivy said. "She meant no harm. I just want to make sure Sophia took no harm."

So did he. He reached the double doors that led to his mother's apartments and opened them.

The rooms had not been used in more than twenty-five years, but the maids dusted and changed the linens regularly, as if anticipating a new marchioness to take up residence. His father had never married again, guests had always been accommodated in other rooms, and Adelaide had wanted to be closer to Kendall's suite.

Now he glanced around the room. In keeping with the Italian theme of the house, the walls were painted in a mural of a Mediterranean countryside, complete with rolling hills, sweeping olive trees, and stone villas. The box bed in the center of the room had gilded cornices shaped like olive fronds, and olive-green ribbon tied back the white and green patterned chintz bed hangings. Small tables on either side of the bed and the wardrobe chest along one wall were lacquered in a more emerald green and painted with gold cranes standing gracefully in shallow blue depths. A mother-of-pearl-backed brush and comb lay waiting on the walnut dressing table.

Ivy rubbed her half-boot against the creamy tuft of the thick carpet. "It's very fine." Her voice was little more than a whisper. "Perhaps I should take Nurse Wilman's room in the nursery. That way we don't have to inconvenience anyone."

"Giving you and Sophia the best is no inconvenience," he told her.

Her lips quirked. "Said the man who has nearly forty staff at his beck and call."

"And pays them well for their trouble," he assured her. "Come look at Weston's room, see if it will do for Sophia."

She joined him at the connecting door and tilted her head to see into the room. She was close enough that her shoulder brushed his. Her head could have rested on his shoulder. How easy to slip his arm about her waist, pull her and Sophia close. He contented himself with admiring the way a strand of hair had come free, like gold curling about her ear.

"Will the crib fit?" she asked.

He forced himself to turn his attention to his brother's room. His brother had had it redecorated when he had come of age, removing anything that might suggest his childhood. Now emerald watered silk covered all the walls and the great walnut bed. The dressing table, highboy dresser, and brace of chairs were also walnut, nearly as brown as the polished wood floor. The only spot of bright was the hearth, surrounded in white marble, like most of the hearths in the house.

"We can remove the bed for now," Kendall said.

"And add a carpet," Ivy suggested. "I would not want my echoing footsteps to be what woke Sophia after finally getting her to sleep. Oh, and bring the rocker, if you please."

She turned to glance his way. For a moment, their gazes brushed. He could not seem to look away.

Sophia shifted in her arms with a sound surprising like the mew of a kitten, and her gaze dropped to the baby.

"Is she all right?" Kendall asked, fear poking at him. Perhaps the rooms outside the nursery really were too cold. Perhaps she did need nourishment. Perhaps he should have left well enough alone.

A soft smile curved Ivy's lips. "She's fallen asleep. Look."

He looked. Dark lashes swept Sophia's cheeks, cheeks that were no longer red from tears. Her rosebud mouth moved in and out, as if she dreamed of eating something tasty. Love washed over him, nearly flattening him in its intensity.

Gulping in air, he stepped back. "I won't disturb her then. I'll have Travis deliver your trunks here and speak to Mrs. Sheppard about the bed, crib, and carpet. No need to change for dinner. We can each take a tray in our rooms."

Something crossed her face. Disappointment? Relief?

"Perhaps that would be best," she agreed. "We've already troubled the staff as it is. Will I see you in the morning?"

"Most likely." And perhaps by then he could get these troublesome emotions under control. It was one thing to feel love for his daughter. What was he to do about the similar feelings that were beginning to crop up, for Ivy?

CHAPTER SEVEN

Julian Mayes leaned back in the chair behind his desk, the legal documents to transfer ownership of an estate out of the hands of a scoundrel scattered across the usually clean surface. Tall bookcases holding the leather-bound volumes of Britain's laws marched in orderly fashion down the walls on either side. If he turned, he might have looked out the window toward St. James's Park.

But the familiar room faded as he considered the future. He was finally going to marry Meredith.

More than ten years—long, lonely years—had passed since she had begged for his proposal under the kissing bough at her mother's annual Christmas Eve party. Her mother had died. Her odious cousin, Nigel—who had inherited her home and everything in it—had refused to support her. Julian had reason to believe Nigel Rose had gone so far as to destroy the notes Meredith had sent him requesting Julian's help, for he had never received them when he had been working as a lowly clerk under the prestigious London solicitor, Sir Alexander Prentice.

Meredith had been forced into serving a cruel mistress, only to be surprised when the lady left her not only a townhouse in London but a sizeable bequest to support it. He had been reunited with his love when she had provided a governess for his friend Alaric, Duke of Wey. And now Alaric and his bride Jane—the former governess—were determined to host Julian and Meredith's wedding.

He had never felt more blessed.

Someone rapped at his door.

"Come in," Julian called.

His clerk put in his head. Sanders was as thin and swift as a greyhound and determined to pursue his career. He bobbed his dark head. "You have a visitor, sir. Sir Alexander Prentice."

Julian rose. "I didn't realize he'd returned. By all means, show him in."

A moment later, and his mentor walked through the door. Alex had always been bigger than life—thick jet-black hair that waved across his brow, piercing blue eyes that could look right through you, broad chest puffed out with justifiable pride. Already a legend in the legal circles of London, he'd been willing to take on a newly minted solicitor from the wilds of Surrey with nothing more to recommend him than a sharp mind and an eager outlook.

Now an extra chin added to the curve of his face, and his waist was nearly as broad as his chest. But his black coat was perfectly tailored, his trousers immaculate, as he came forward to clasp Julian's outstretched hand.

"Alex, good to see you. When did you get back?"

"A few days ago," he admitted, releasing Julian to seat himself on one of the chairs opposite Julian's desk. "It was a near-run thing. The declaration of war came just after we set sail from Baltimore. I kept expecting a privateer to blow us out of the water."

"Yet here you are," Julian said, taking the chair beside him. "What will do you now? Does Liverpool intend to keep you on the negotiations with our cousins across the sea?"

"The Prime Minister has other plans in that area, alas," Alex said, adjusting one of the shining gold buttons on his wine-colored waistcoat. "For the moment, I am catching up with a few long-term clients, such as the Marquess of

NEVER MARRY A MARQUESS 65

Kendall. I believe you recently stood up at his wedding."

Julian smiled. "I did."

"Then I suppose I have you to thank for drawing up the marriage settlements. My staff disclaimed all knowledge."

Julian leaned back in his chair. "Lord Kendall never approached me."

Alex shook his head. "The young fool. I might have known he'd jump into marriage again without another thought. Top over teakettle in love like the last time, no doubt. But then, his father was alive and made sure the proper arrangements were made. What do you know of his bride?"

"Miss Ivy Bateman is a very pleasant young lady," Julian assured him. "I am familiar with her family and her brother, Sir Matthew."

Alex relaxed, but only the slightest. "A gentleman's daughter, then."

He had to go carefully. Meredith was remarkably open-minded, and loyal, when it came to her ladies. While Julian had never been entirely sure of her role in Ivy Bateman's marriage, he knew she'd had a hand.

"Her brother was recently elevated for services to the crown. He saved His Royal Highness's life."

Alex frowned. "Do you speak of that balloon incident? The news was even in the Baltimore paper. But I thought the fellow who saved him was some pugilist. The Beast of Birmingham, wasn't it? Hardly quality."

"Miss Bateman is lovely, cultured, and the kindest person I have ever met," Julian informed him. "Lord Kendall seems sincerely fond of her."

"They generally are," Alex said darkly. He sighed. "If only he'd written to me. I would have advised him to stay away. He is in no position to take a bride."

Julian frowned. "A marquess possessed of a good fortune and a respectable family name would seem to be in an excellent position to marry again."

"Perhaps not as much as you think," Alex replied. "His income is largely tied up in investments. I've had to manage his money carefully. She married the wrong man if she is hoping to make free with his funds."

The bald statement poked him in the chest, but Julian did not react. He had learned to hide his thoughts over the years. It was never wise to show dismay when a respected client approached bankruptcy, nor to gloat when a particularly loathsome client ignored Julian's advice and found himself in a difficult position. He would not allow Alex to see the distaste his comment engendered.

"As I said, I have been impressed with Ivy Bateman's character," he said. "Whatever agreement she and Lord Kendall reached is likely more than reasonable."

"If Kendall isn't so besotted he'd offer her anything." He shook his head. "I cannot like the changes in Society since I left. Carrolton married some French countess who was his mother's companion. Worthington wed that Villers chit whose brother was forever pushing her forward. Promise me you will be wiser."

He should not be so perversely delighted about nettling his mentor, but he couldn't help it. "Wish me happy, old man. I'm soon to marry Meredith Thorn."

Alex stared at him. "Thorn? You must know that isn't her real name."

Julian nodded. "I met her years ago, when she went by Mary Rose."

"Then you know she's a murderess."

Cold settled over him. "I know no such thing."

"Oh, she was never formally charged, because the rightful heir decided to settle his concerns out of court," Alex allowed. "But I had no doubt she pushed Lady Winhaven into the fit that claimed her life."

"Then it's a good thing I'm marrying her and you aren't," Julian said with some asperity.

Alex pushed himself upright. "Those lavender eyes have

bewitched you. Jilt her at once. It's the only way."

Julian refused to rise and meet the fellow's outraged gaze. "I can see why you might be concerned, Alex, but you are mistaken in Meredith. She is the finest woman it has been my privilege to know. You think her a fortune hunter. Do you know what she did with the money Lady Winhaven left her? She opened an employment agency for gentlewomen down on their luck. The Duke of Wey's wife was one of her clients. So are Lady Carrolton, Lady Orwell, Lady Worthington, and, I suspect, the new Lady Kendall."

Alex threw up his hands. "You see? That only proves my point. What you suggest as noble I know as avarice. Her strategy is obvious. She is worming her way into good Society by placing her clients strategically and aligning herself with a trusted member of the legal profession. You are merely a pawn in her game."

Julian forced himself up at last. "Alex, I will not have you speak about my intended this way."

Immediately his former mentor's face softened. Alex put a hand on his shoulder, the touch both possessive and heavy. "Then I will say no more. But you are the one mistaken, my friend. I cannot help but feel myself responsible for not exposing her years ago."

"Alex," Julian began in warning, but the older solicitor released him to turn for the door.

"Do not concern yourself," he told Julian with a wave of his meaty hand. "I have much to do now that I've returned. You will hear from me shortly."

And he was out the door before Julian could stop him.

Sophia's cries had Ivy up three times during the night. The second time Becky ran to the kitchen for gruel.

The other occasions a few minutes of walking, chewing on a dampened silk handkerchief, and a lullaby had been enough to soothe the baby back to sleep. A shame Ivy couldn't return to slumber so easily. The massive bed with its gilded coverings, elaborate draperies, and deep mattress felt foreign. Her thoughts chased each other across the thick covers.

Kendall had been right. Sophia desperately needed a mother, someone to put her first. That would not be so difficult for Ivy. But how was she to deal with Mrs. Sheppard and all these servants? Kendall took them for granted. She could not.

A dark-haired, fine-boned maid about Ivy's age had unpacked her trunks and helped her change for bed. Her name was Percy, and it had taken some doing on Ivy's part to convince her to admit as much. Ivy still wasn't sure if that was the maid's first name or her last. It seemed marchionesses were not to converse with their maids. And Percy had merely bobbed a curtsey, frowning, when Ivy told her what time to return in the morning. Apparently, marchionesses were not supposed to be up and about by seven either.

Becky had no trouble with the hour. Ivy found her in Sophia's room, the baby in her arms, when she came through the connecting door at a quarter past.

"I opened the draperies and dressed her for the day," she reported in a rush as she curtsied. "That's what you wanted, wasn't it, your ladyship?"

"Yes, thank you," Ivy said, moving closer. "Now, perhaps we could find a way of feeding her something more substantial than gruel."

Becky nodded to the walnut dressing table, which now held a silver tray set with small, patterned bowls of delicate porcelain. "Mrs. Sheppard talked to Mrs. Grunion, our cook. She sent up mashes. I didn't know what to do with them."

Ivy beckoned her over, and together they gazed down at the offerings. The green was likely peas, the orange carrots. She stuck a finger in the white.

"Cauliflower," she reported. "Let's see which she prefers."

The little girl stared solemnly at the food as Becky sat with her beside the table. Sophia's hair, eyes, and complexion must have come from her mother, but that concerned look was all her father. Every time he smiled, the air tasted sweeter. When did he rise and breakfast?

Likely later than now. The house was entirely too quiet. Ivy reached for one of the tiny silver spoons the cook had sent up. She put some of the cauliflower on the tip and held it before Sophia's mouth. The baby nearly crossed her eyes trying to focus on it.

"Open up, little bird," Ivy encouraged her. She bumped the spoon gently against Sophia's lips, mindful of the tooth just behind. Sophia opened her mouth, and in went the cauliflower. Her eyes widened. She rolled the mash around her mouth, licked her lips, and swallowed.

"She ate it," Becky said, sounding awed.

She ate several spoonsful before Ivy switched to carrots. Those met with equal success. But one mouthful of the peas, and Sophia's face wrinkled.

"Never was one for mushy peas myself," Becky confessed.

"One more bite," Ivy urged, bringing the spoon forward. The peas went in, and Sophia pushed them out with her tongue. The green dribbled down her little chin and plopped onto her beribboned gown.

"It wasn't my fault," Becky said, her own face pinching.

Sophia started whimpering.

"No need for concern," Ivy assured the maid, setting aside the spoon to take the baby from her trembling grip. "I'll clean her up. You return the tray to the kitchen and tell the cook I'll be down to talk to her shortly."

Becky picked up the tray and fled.

In short order, Ivy had cleaned Sophia up and readied

her for the day. She carried the little girl down the white marble stairs to the entry hall. The blond-haired Travis was on duty, looking at bit like ash in his grey coat against all the white marble.

"Which way to the kitchen, if you please?" Ivy asked. "I need to speak to the cook."

Travis kept his gaze straight ahead as he stood tall and proud by the front door. "I'd be happy to fetch the cook for you, your ladyship."

Ivy frowned. "Why would I interrupt her work any more than necessary?"

He started, then moved away from the door. "Allow me to show you the way, your ladyship."

Ivy fell into step beside him. He never looked at her directly, but she saw him glancing down at Lady Sophia in her arms. Had he never seen the baby before? He certainly had heard her, if yesterday was any indication. Now Sophia stared solemnly back at him, as if just as perplexed.

He led them out of the entry hall into an east-facing paneled corridor that quickly turned north. She was surprised to see light coming from wide windows on her right, where the inside of the house should be.

"What's that?" she asked, peering into a wide, well-lit space.

"That's the pavement room," he said.

Sophia wiggled her little lips as if considering speaking the words aloud.

Ivy did speak them aloud. "The pavement room?"

He stopped, glanced both ways, then leaned forward and lowered his voice. "Villa Romanesque is like a big circle, only it's square. In the center is where the Roman things are kept. The pavement room is open all the way to the top, where it's covered by glass." He shrugged as he straightened, as if to show he couldn't understand the vagaries of the rich and titled.

"I see," Ivy said. That must be where Kendall kept the

mosaic he'd talked about on the way here. She'd have to ask for a tour later.

The corridor ended in a wall covered in a mural like the one in her room. She didn't notice the latch until he'd reached for it and opened the door the mural concealed. The scents of a busy kitchen wafted out to her. He went ahead of her to stand in the doorway of the kitchen proper and announce, "Her ladyship, the Marchioness of Kendall, and Lady Sophia."

Everyone stopped. Indeed, a metal bowl fell with a clang that echoed in the high-ceilinged room. She counted half a dozen people scattered around the large kitchen, from the pot boy about Tuny's age scrubbing pans in the big porcelain sink under the window to the ample woman with her sleeves rolled up before the massive oak table in the center of the room. She wiped off her hands and hurried up to Ivy, dropping a curtsey that made her requisite grey skirts bunch on the flagstone floor.

"Your ladyship. Is there a problem?"

Why did they all assume the worst? "No, not at all," Ivy promised her. "I merely wanted your advice."

The woman reared back, setting her blond hair flying under the edges of her ruffled cap. "*My* advice?"

"Yes," Ivy said, aware that every gaze was turned her way. "The food you sent up for Sophia was perfect. For now, I thought one type of food at a setting, cauliflower or carrots. Peas did not go over well, but we'll try them again in a few days. Perhaps you could recommend what else available here in Surrey to add to the rotation."

"Yes, your ladyship."

She was so wary. Ivy pressed ahead anyway. "I know you must focus on the large meals for the adults and the staff. If you'll tell me your cooking schedule, I'll endeavor to put Sophia on an eating regimen that doesn't conflict."

The cook frowned, peering closer at her, grey eyes narrowing. "You're offering to arrange your schedule to meet mine?"

"Certainly," Ivy said. "You have challenging, important work to do to feed everyone on this estate. I wouldn't dream of interfering with that."

The cook's mouth dropped.

The door banged open behind them, and Mrs. Sheppard hurried into the room. "Forgive me, your ladyship," she said. "I didn't realize you expected to discuss domestic arrangements this morning." She came around Ivy, her gaze falling to the baby in her arms. She jerked to a stop. "Where is Becky Bradley? Why isn't she at her post?"

"Here, mum. Sorry, mum." Becky edged her way into sight from the back of the room, where she must have been putting away the cleaned dishes from Sophia's breakfast.

"I sent Becky to the kitchen," Ivy explained before the lightning could flash from the thunderclouds gathering on the housekeeper's face. "She's been nothing but a blessing this morning."

Mrs. Sheppard's color receded. "Very good, then. And what has Mrs. Grunion done to displease?"

"Nothing," Ivy hurried to assure her as the cook shut her mouth and paled. "We were just discussing the most efficient way to work Sophia's diet into the cooking schedule."

"She offered to let me set the schedule to my convenience," the cook informed the housekeeper, as if Ivy had suggested they all take a trip to the moon.

"How benevolent," Mrs. Sheppard said. "We'll need to speak to his lordship before making any changes, of course."

The cook nodded, settling on her feet as if order had been restored.

It seemed she'd blundered. She was so used to dealing with Anna, their maid of all work and the only servant she'd had for years, she hadn't considered the hierarchy in such a large staff. "Forgive me, Mrs. Sheppard," she said. "I should have realized I should speak to you first."

Now they were all gaping, and Ivy's face felt hot. Sophia's face puckered as if she sensed the tension building.

"Perhaps, when you have an opportunity, we could speak," Ivy continued to the housekeeper. She turned for the door, only wanting to escape, and her gaze lit on a massive scarlet circle of metal built into the white marble hearth.

Something inside her leaped up, reached out, cried for joy.

"You have an oven," Ivy breathed.

Mrs. Grunion straightened with evident pride. "We do indeed. We bake our own breads and pastries."

And cinnamon buns. She loved baking cinnamon buns. No one was sad or embarrassed or dismayed over a cinnamon bun and a cup of tea. At their home in Birmingham and Matthew's house, she had been confined to a cast iron oven pressed into the coals of the fire. Think what she could do with such a marvel as this!

She glanced from the cook to the housekeeper, both of whom were frowning at her. Marchionesses weren't apparently supposed to talk to the cook. They weren't supposed to clean up after babies either. They wouldn't bake cinnamon buns or take joy from serving them.

But the scarlet door was whispering her name, promising untold delights. Anise biscuits, proper cakes, popovers, hot cross buns for Easter next year.

She raised her head and addressed herself to the housekeeper. "I intend to bake, at least every other day. I'll need flour, finely sifted; white sugar, scraped and pounded; cinnamon grated; yeast or starter; milk; and freshly churned butter. I'll let you know a day in advance if other ingredients are required. Is nine in the morning convenient for you?"

Mrs. Grunion and Mrs. Sheppard exchanged glances.

"Your ladyship, there is no need," the housekeeper began.

There was every need. The staff were downcast and worried. Kendall rarely smiled. Even Sophia, when she could chew, would benefit from a treat once in a while.

"I intend to bake," Ivy repeated. "Lord Kendall said you were to obey me in all things. I will demand little, will do all I can not to inconvenience you. But I will not be gainsaid in this."

Mrs. Sheppard met her gaze. "I'm not sure Lord Kendall will approve."

"Then Lord Kendall," Ivy said, "will not be told."

Someone gasped and was hushed. Sophia turned to look at Mrs. Sheppard, screwed up her rosebud lips, stuck out her tongue, and blew bubbles, loudly.

Mrs. Sheppard blinked.

"Tomorrow at nine," Ivy said to the cook. "See that you have pans appropriately sized for the oven. Becky can watch Sophia for a short time so I can bake. I will see you then."

CHAPTER EIGHT

Kendall had dressed, taken his ride in the cool of the summer morning, and breakfasted. The house felt odd, and it was a moment before he realized why. It was entirely too quiet. He had one foot on the stairs to go up to the nursery when he remembered Sophia was no longer there. He stepped down into the chamber floor and glanced down the other end of the corridor. An invisible wall hovered between him and Ivy's suite.

Ridiculous! This was his home. Ivy was his partner. There was no reason he couldn't visit his daughter. He marched himself to the door of his brother's old room and opened it.

The staff had removed his brother's bed and replaced it with Sophia's crib. The rocker rested near the hearth. But he heard nothing of his daughter or Ivy.

Becky looked up from sweeping the carpet, eyes wide. "Yes, your lordship? Did you need something?"

"Where are Sophia and her ladyship?" he asked.

She gripped the broom tighter, as if she thought he'd take it from her. "She carried Lady Sophia off somewhere. She said something about sunlight."

Sunlight? Outdoors? What would heat and wind do to his fragile daughter? What about bees? Poisonous snakes? Brigands! He pelted out of the room and careened down the stairs.

"Lady Kendall?" he demanded of the underfootman on duty beside the door.

The young man hurried to open the front door for him. "In the north garden, my lord."

The north garden, the one with the stone fountain at the center. What if Sophia fell in and drowned? How could he face Adelaide in heaven one day if he were the cause of their daughter's death?

He skidded across the gravel drive, leaped the first low hedge into the garden, and barely managed to pull himself up as he sighted the fountain.

Ivy stood at the intersection of four of the paths through the garden, next to the curved white stone of the fountain. Though she wore no bonnet, she had found one for Sophia, the soft white fabric forming a cap that protected her face from the summer sun. Her long cotton frock protected her body as well. As Kendall watched, Ivy moved close enough to the fountain that she could put her hand under the falling water, murmuring to Sophia. His daughter reached out her tiny fingers, touched the glittering liquid.

Sophia giggled.

The sound of her joy nearly dropped him to his knees. Had he ever heard such delight before? How could he hear it more often? He made himself approach slowly, carefully, lest he startle her.

Ivy glanced up and smiled. "Good morning, my lord. Lovely day for a stroll."

And it was. The blue sky was dotted with fluffy white clouds. The gentlest of breezes brushed his cheek, bringing with it the scent of roses. In her white muslin dress, blond hair confined behind her head, Ivy looked as if she were meant to be here.

"Good morning," he greeted her. "How are my two beauties today?" He bent to see under the brim of Sophia's bonnet.

Two blue eyes gazed back at him. Then she pursed her

lips, stuck out her tongue, and made a rude noise.

Kendall reared back.

"She discovered that sound this morning," Ivy told him with an amused smile as his daughter giggled again. "I expect we'll hear it often before she tires of it. Daisy still occasionally blows bubbles at me."

His daughter threw out one hand and wiggled as if determined to feel the water again.

He couldn't believe the change in Sophia. For so long, she had lain listless in her crib, staring at nothing. That was, if she wasn't crying. Everyone had all but despaired of her.

Now she made rude noises and laughed. He could imagine some would not be pleased.

He had never felt so happy.

"A mermaid, are we?" Ivy asked Sophia. "Perhaps we can give you a proper bath later. Indoors, of course," she added as if she'd seen the concern creeping back onto Kendall's face.

And why had he been so concerned? There was nothing here to harm Sophia. He could trust Ivy. Wasn't that one of the reasons he'd married her?

"And what do you have planned after your stroll?" he asked as she turned away from the fountain.

"Sitting," Ivy said.

She made it sound an impressive feat. "Sitting?" he asked as they strolled through the garden, the sun warm on his hair.

"On the carpet, I think," Ivy replied. "Sophia leaned too heavily against Becky this morning at breakfast."

He frowned. "Isn't that natural when being fed the bottle?"

"Oh, she didn't rely on a bottle," Ivy said with a smile at the little girl in her arms. "She ate food like a big girl." She looked knowingly at Kendall. "Cauliflower."

He tried to imagine his daughter chewing the vegetable. "Is that wise?"

"She liked it very well. Carrots too. See how they put a bloom in her cheeks?"

He could not deny it. Sophia's eyes glowed as she took in the world around her. Still, sitting on a carpet. On the floor. What if she toppled over, struck her head against the hardwood at the edge of the carpet? What if some dirt from the carpet reached her hands, was transferred to her mouth? Was that why Becky was sweeping, to prevent such a calamity? Would she be thorough enough?

"I'll come with you," he said, turning back toward the house.

She cast him a glance. "If it pleases you. Do not marquesses have important matters that must be attended to?"

A letter from the opposition leader on bills he hoped to enter into discussion next term, a report from his land steward on the state of his properties, a request from the Duke of Wey to consider joining in the construction of a new weir to further curtail flooding along the Thames. Minor matters compared to the health of his daughter.

"Nothing urgent at the moment," he assured Ivy.

Sophia blew bubbles at him.

He thought they would ascend to the new nursery as soon as they entered the house, but Ivy turned to the left. "Perhaps you could show us the pavement room, my lord."

He frowned. "Now? Isn't it better for Sophia to retire to her room after such an exertion?"

"Exertion? I merely carried her around the garden." With one hand, she tugged at the ribbon tied under Sophia's chin and pulled off the bonnet. Ebony curls gleamed in the sunlight coming through the window.

Adelaide's curls. Adelaide's daughter.

"Perhaps another time," he said, reaching for Sophia. "I'd like to see how she sits."

Ivy cocked her head, eyeing him. Then she straightened and accompanied him up the stairs to the safety of the new nursery.

But it was no safer here; he saw that immediately. The legs of the dressing table had been planted on a portion of the new carpet. What if she fell against them? Worse, what if the table should topple over on her? Handing her back to Ivy, he shoved the table along the wall until it was off the carpet. Then he pulled a quilt out of the crib and wrapped it over the stone hearth. Becky, standing near the window, looked at him as if he'd gone mad. She scrambled aside as he approached to loop the curtains up onto the sill. Wouldn't want Sophia to tug on them and pull them down on her. She might smother before he could come to her rescue.

"There," he said, turning to survey his work. "You may safely set her on the carpet."

Ivy's mouth twitched, but she didn't smile as she bent to lay his daughter on the floor on her belly. He had to stand ramrod straight to prevent himself from reaching for Sophia.

The baby lifted her head from the carpet, but her frown suggested she didn't like the view. She lay down again and rolled onto her back to stare up at the ceiling. Kendall glanced up as well. His brother's old room had one of the few undecorated ceilings in the house. He'd bring in an artist to fix that. What should it be for Sophia? Clouds? Cherubs? A pastoral scene?

"Well, will you look at that?" Becky marveled.

He dropped his gaze to find that his daughter had risen to her hands and knees and was rocking back and forth as if she couldn't decide whether to go forward or scoot toward the wall. Ivy was beaming as if she couldn't be prouder. He knew the feeling.

Sophia lifted a hand, and he crouched on the floor a few feet from her. "That's my girl. Come to Papa."

She leaned forward and plopped onto her face on the carpet.

Blood congealing, he rushed to lift her even as her eyes

pooled with tears. "Fetch Doctor Penrose," he demanded, and Becky flew toward the door.

"Stop," Ivy ordered. She swept up to him and peered into Sophia's face. His daughter's attempt at a smile showed her new tooth to advantage.

"She's fine, Kendall," Ivy said gently. "Babies need to explore."

Not his daughter. She needed to be safe, protected. "She can explore some other time." He carried her carefully to her crib and laid her down on her back. She gazed up at him as he straightened. Then her lips trembled, and two fat tears slid down from her beautiful eyes.

"Is she in pain?" Kendall asked, heart twisting inside him. Ivy came to join him. Sophia held out her arms.

"No," Ivy said. "She is coming to understand her world is bigger than these bars. She is no longer content to hide behind them. She should be encouraged."

"She should be kept safe," Kendall argued, stepping back, fear and duty battling inside him. "We cannot push her beyond endurance."

Ivy eyed him. "Her endurance or yours?"

Kendall raised his head. "My endurance has nothing to do with the matter. I am beyond delighted at her progress thus far, Ivy. I just don't want to see her hurt. Now, if you'll excuse me, there are some matters this marquess must attend to." He turned and left the room, with the unsettling feeling that he was running away.

Well! If it wasn't enough Nurse Wilman had nearly smothered the baby, now Kendall refused to allow her to grow. Ivy gazed down at Sophia in her crib. The little girl rolled onto her stomach and raised herself up, but there wasn't any room to move. She slumped back down with an audible sigh.

"Should I pick her up?" Becky asked from the other side of the crib, face pinched with concern.

Kendall wouldn't like it. But he'd asked Ivy to marry him so she could take care of his daughter. Allowing her to remain weak, helpless, was no way to care for her.

"Yes," Ivy said. "Take her to the rocker, and see if she wants to nap."

Becky did as she was bid.

That made one of them.

Ivy leaned against the crib and watched the nursemaid rock the baby slowly. Why was Kendall so protective? He'd called his daughter frail, and she was small for her age. But Ivy had been with Sophia less than twenty-four hours and already the baby had proven resilient. She certainly wasn't at death's door. Ivy's mother and father had never treated Daisy as if she were made of thin glass. Even Mrs. Bateman, who had spoiled Tuny something terrible, had not coddled her so much. Ivy and her sisters had had chores since they had been old enough to undertake a responsibility. Lady Sophia would only have to raise her pretty little hand before a servant came to fulfill her every wish.

But first she had to raise her hand.

So did Ivy. She couldn't just sit around. She wasn't used to idleness. She straightened and busied herself gathering up the things for the laundry, smoothing the blankets in the crib. Becky hummed a tuneless lullaby, head bent over the baby in her arms. Sophia yawned, then cuddled closer, then relaxed in sleep. Becky looked up at Ivy wide-eyed, as if amazed at what she'd done.

Ivy tipped her head toward the crib, and Becky came to lay the baby down. They both stood watching her a moment.

"She's almost like a real baby now," Becky said.

Ivy motioned her back from the crib and led her into the other room.

"A real baby?" she asked.

Becky dropped her gaze and shuffled her feet under her grey skirts. "Yes, your ladyship. Seems like all she did was cry before you came. Babies shouldn't cry that much. It's not natural."

Very likely not. Too many things had conspired to keep Sophia in such a state. Nurse Wilman had mentioned colic. Now the baby was teething. Perhaps there had been the usual ills that attended infants—ear aches, fevers. All the more reason to celebrate her health now.

And with Sophia napping, Ivy had a few precious minutes on her hands. She had never appreciated the social whirl in London, but she refused to be kept in two rooms for the rest of her life. At home, before Charlotte had tried to make her into a Society lady, she would have helped with the cleaning, baked for dinner and breakfast the next morning, done the laundry, or worked on the mending. A marchioness did none of those things, and she'd promised she wouldn't bake until tomorrow morning. Unlike in London, there were no invitations from friends expecting a response, no park in which she could promenade. Kendall must have a library.

And then there was the pavement room. It truly had been the most intriguing thing she'd seen in the house so far. Surely no one would mind if she took a closer look.

"Stay with her," Ivy said. "Send word when she wakes."

Becky nodded, and Ivy slipped out into the corridor.

She followed the path to the room easily enough, gently refusing the footman's offer of help. Pushing open the glass-paned door, she stepped inside.

Time fell away.

All around her, white marble statues posed—a youth with a disk of some kind, arm cocked as if he would send it hurtling across the potted ferns at his feet; a mother with a babe in her arms, face wistful as she looked to the future; a warrior leaning on his spear, weary of battle; a maiden, hair down and arms up in praise of her Creator. Terracotta tiles made a path through their silent village, while high overhead, the glass dome sent sunlight down to anoint brow and shoulder. Somewhere she heard the tinkle of water falling: a fountain, most likely.

She should bring Sophia here.

Would he allow it?

She could see nothing that might endanger the child as she wandered the path, hand touching a stone hip here and sculpted foot there, skirts brushing the dusky green leaves of the potted plants. Ahead, the space between the statues widened to a square perhaps ten feet on a side. Ivy approached to stare.

The wood floor had been left open to the ground, which lay a foot or so below the edges. Inside, tiny square tiles were pressed into the dirt—pure white and deep blue and rich copper—to form a mosaic of a flower with waves encircling it. Cool air brought up the scent of earth and water. She knelt and reached out a hand.

"Careful. It's very old."

She straightened to find Kendall coming up behind her. He didn't seem concerned that she would touch the pavement below. Indeed, his face glowed as he stopped beside her.

"This is Roman," he said, "left by those who first built here. It's a link to the ancient past, a reminder that we are not alone in this life."

"May I?" Ivy asked.

He nodded, and she bent again, her fingers tracing the pattern on the rough tile. "And people walked on this, hundreds of years ago?"

"More than fifteen hundred years ago," he murmured, crouching beside her. "Before there was ever a king of England."

She pulled back her hand, awe rising inside her. "You are right to protect it."

His eyes were bright with light and purpose. "It is an honor and a duty."

So fervent, so dedicated. She had only seen the look one other time.

When he was gazing at Sophia.

That was what he did, that is what he believed—that if you loved, you protected. But there was so much difference between an ancient pavement and a little girl.

And a wife.

She had come to Villa Romanesque to help Sophia. But his response to his daughter and this marvelous mosaic proved he had a heart deep enough to care.

Could she help him see the need to step back, allow Sophia to grow?

Noble ambition, but she had another, one she'd been holding inside since the day she'd first been introduced to him.

Could she encourage him to care for her?

CHAPTER NINE

K endall was used to the responses to the pavement. He remembered the first time his father had brought him into the room, allowed him to touch the ancient stones, fewer then. He could still feel the grit of the dirt under his fingers as he and his father had brushed off the edges to reveal the full extent of the work. The former Duke of Wey and his son the current duke, the Earl of Carrolton to the east of him, and dozens of other guests had all talked in hushed tones, faces registering awe, wonder. Ivy had looked the same way when he'd come upon her, her brown eyes wide.

But now she had turned her gaze on him, and it held no less wonder. A man could accustom himself to such looks.

He straightened. "Were you seeking me? You had only to ring for a footman."

She lifted her skirts to rise. He offered a hand to help. She didn't appear to notice, for she didn't accept it. "Your family built all this to protect these tiles? Are the statues as old?"

"No," Kendall admitted. "Most are copies of ancient pieces, commissioned by my grandfather and father. They felt strongly that such works should remain in the countries where they were created. A few are new works." He waved a hand to direct her toward the statue to the right of the pavement, surrounded by vases of flowers that were replenished daily from the conservatory. "This was my mother."

Ivy gazed at the white marble. Kendall had looked at the statue so many times over the years. At first, he'd searched for similarities—the wave of her hair, the shape of her eyes, so like his own. Later he'd tried in vain to spot any kind of emotion. His father had vowed that Kendall's mother had loved him with a fierce devotion. She had been credited with nursing Wes through the illness that would take her own life. She was a legend, the pinnacle of motherly art.

But the statue kept his mother's secrets well. The only sign of expression was a slight frown as she directed her gaze toward the pavement that had been her husband's pride.

"I see where you favor her," Ivy said. She turned to the next statue of a young woman. "And who is this?"

This statue highlighted emotion. Hair curled around her delicate face, the woman beamed at the world. He could almost see the mischievous sparkle in her eyes. But he couldn't stand gazing at it. It was cold, lifeless.

"That is Adelaide," he said. "My wife."

She recoiled. "I didn't realize…"

He took her arm and led her toward the door, memories chasing him. "It was a gift from her parents for our first anniversary. Adelaide died before seeing it. I didn't want to hurt her parents' feelings by refusing it."

"Will they be hurt because you married me?"

Her voice held concern, sympathy. He had never met anyone so kind. "No. We lost them shortly after Sophia was born. Influenza, the physician said, but I'm not sure they had the will to go on after losing Adelaide. She was their only child, born late in their marriage. She was everything to them."

"To you too, I think," she murmured.

He felt as if she'd brushed dirt off his heart to expose it as surely as he had exposed the pavement. "She was. But enough of such talk. What did you need of me?"

They had reached the door, and he ushered her through and shut it firmly behind him. She paused in the corridor.

"I wasn't searching for you. Sophia is napping. I thought to explore the house. It is my home now."

Of course it was her house. A wife had every right to expect her husband to introduce her to it. He had been so focused on Sophia, he had forgotten about Ivy's needs.

He swept her a bow. "Lady Kendall, allow me to show you your home. I have some little familiarity with it."

He straightened to find her eyes soft. "I can imagine no finer guide, sir. Lead on."

She took his offered arm. How well she fit beside him, her head nearly as tall as his. Dressed in silk, his mother's jewels at her neck and in her hair, she would be a formidable marchioness.

Your mother's jewels belong to your wife, the nagging voice in his head insisted. *You gave them to Adelaide and saved them for Sophia. You cannot take them back.*

He forced himself to open the double doors across from the pavement room. "This is the Emperor's Hall. We use it on formal occasions."

She glanced around at all the gilded molding, the alabaster urns nearly her height, the carpet woven to represent the head of Caesar from a coin his father had seen on his Grand Tour of the Continent. "Do we host formal occasions often?"

"No," he admitted, closing the door and escorting her down the corridor. "And this is the conservatory. We grow flowers year-round and oranges, lemons, and strawberries."

They stepped into the glass-walled room, and the humidity wrapped around him like a blanket.

"Pineapple?" she asked, voice oddly breathless, as if something more than the humidity had affected her.

"Three plants, brought back from the other side of the world. Mrs. Grunion uses them for ices."

"And cakes," Ivy said, gaze as far away as the plant's home. "The icing would be marvelous."

Kendall stuck out his lower lip. "Perhaps you could advise her on what you'd like."

She returned to him and smiled. "Perhaps."

He led her through the rest of the ground floor and the first floor, surprised by how many times he explained that the room was seldom used. How long had it been since Villa Romanesque had known life, joy? He wanted to draw back the drapes, throw open every window, let in the light. Just as Ivy had done in his daughter's life.

At length, they reached Sophia's new nursery, but Ivy stopped him before he could open the door. "What do you expect from me, Kendall?" she asked, gaze searching his.

"To devote yourself to Sophia," he replied, "as we agreed."

"Surely you know that will not take all my time," she protested. "You must have had some idea of my role."

In truth, he hadn't thought any farther than his daughter. He hadn't even considered where Ivy would sleep! Mrs. Sheppard had managed the household since he had returned from Eton. Adelaide had done little to interfere with her.

He spread his hands. "This is your home, Ivy, as you noted. Do whatever pleases you."

She eyed him a moment, as if doubting his word, then inclined her head. "Very well, Kendall, but remember you said that. I am not sure what pleases me will be what should please a marchioness."

Ivy managed to have everything in place so she could bake the next morning. Kendall had said she should do as she pleased, but she still doubted he'd approve if he knew. She made sure Sophia was settled first. Breakfast had been successful: carrots this time, with minimum spills on Sophia's pretty pink gown. She would have to see about making bibs, if marchionesses were allowed that little task. Becky was going to clean her up and then take her on a walk about the house, staying away from the pavement and the conservatory. Ivy had a feeling the mere mention of Sophia and those rooms would make Kendall twitch.

"But come fetch me if there is any issue," she stressed as she and the nursemaid descended the stairs, Sophia up in Becky's arms and twisting to take in everything they passed, from the gold crowning the columns to the landscape paintings gracing the walls.

"Yes, your ladyship," Becky said, treading carefully as if she knew she carried the most important person in the house.

The staff went rigid again when Ivy walked in the kitchen door, but she decided to pay them no mind. So long as she didn't get in anyone's way, they would likely become accustomed to her in time. Mrs. Grunion had bowls and ingredients and pans spread out on the end of the massive work table, closest to the oven.

"The oven has been heated, and the coals swept out, your ladyship," she reported. Then her thick-fingered hands laced in front of her. "Do you need any assistance?" Her brows were so tight in concern she puckered her forehead below her cap.

Ivy began rolling up the sleeves on her white muslin gown. "Just an apron, thank you. I know what I'm doing."

The cook's sniff said otherwise.

Ivy couldn't care. It was easy to lose herself in the measuring and mixing, the cool, springy texture of the dough as she kneaded it. Leaving it to rise, she buttered her pans, marveling at the shiny surface. Her pans at home were dull, battered. She knew how each dent had been earned—the first time Tuny had helped and dropped the buttered pan on the floor, the time Daisy had tried to cram a pan into the cupboard so Matthew wouldn't guess what they had been baking for his birthday. Perhaps one day she and Sophia would put dents in these pans.

She snorted and looked away from Mrs. Grunion's frown. Sophia would never be allowed to bake. If Kendall found sitting on the carpet frightfully dangerous, he would have apoplexy over a heated oven. Which meant Ivy had to find a way past his defenses.

And the cook's. Mrs. Grunion continued to hover as Ivy punched down the dough, then rolled it out and sprinkled it with cinnamon and sugar. But two hours later, the cook was the first to crowd around the oven as Ivy took out her cinnamon buns, and this time, any sniffs sounded decidedly eager.

Ivy lay the pans on the work table, cinnamon skipping through the air and satisfaction lifting her heart. The edges were golden brown, the swirls dark with spice. She might be a marchioness now, but she still knew her craft. And the oven was such a blessing!

"Mrs. Grunion," she said, "please send up four for his lordship and me for a mid-morning treat and serve the rest to the staff."

The cook clutched her chest, eyes widening. "Oh, your ladyship. How kind."

Ivy smiled. "It's not kind to do what I love, but I hope you all enjoy them as much as my family did. Perhaps Naples biscuits on Thursday. Sophia might enjoy gnawing on them."

"I'll have the ingredients ready," the cook promised, gaze straying to the steaming buns.

Ivy removed her apron, tucked a few strands of heat-limp hair back into her arrangement, and went in search of Becky and Sophia.

She found them in the nursery, with Kendall. Sophia was once more in her crib and crying this time, the whimpers clinging to the walls.

"What happened?" she asked, hurrying closer.

Becky shrunk in on herself.

Kendall crossed his arms over his chest, widening the shoulders of his bottle green coat. "I found them in the library," he informed Ivy with a look to Becky. "Looking at books."

Oh, dear. Ivy swallowed. "Were the books very rare and expensive?"

Kendall lowered his arms. "No, not at all."

Ivy regarded him. "Then they must have been urgently needed by someone else on the estate."

"No," he allowed. "But surely you see the problem, Ivy. If there had been any sort of tremor, the bookcases might have fallen on Sophia."

"Tremors. I see." Ivy made herself look concerned. "Forgive me. I haven't studied the geology of Surrey. Are we prone to tremors here?"

"Never saw one in my lifetime," Becky muttered.

"No," Kendall said again. "But one can't be too careful."

Once more that fierce protectiveness surged up inside her. Perhaps he felt it too to keep Sophia so swaddled. Ivy could not allow him to continue. "Yes," she told him, "one can be entirely too careful. One can be so careful that one's daughter shrivels away into a listless, lifeless husk. Is that what you want?"

He stiffened away from her. "Ivy! Of course not."

"Good." Ivy reached into the crib and picked up the baby. "Then hold your daughter and tell her you're sorry."

He blinked at her as she held out Sophia. The baby wiggled as if eager to greet her father, and Kendall seized her as if terrified Ivy would drop her. Sophia eyed him solemnly.

"Apologize," Ivy said.

He frowned. "I will do no such thing. She doesn't even know what I'm saying."

The little girl might not talk yet, but those blue eyes missed little.

"Sophia," Ivy said, pointing toward the spindles of the crib. "Do you want to go back into your crib?"

Sophia shrank against her father, clutching at his arm for dear life.

"Talk to her," Ivy urged. "She understands more than you know."

Still, he frowned at the baby. Sophia blew bubbles at him. His frown evaporated.

"Think you're clever, do you?" he said. And he stuck his tongue out and blew bubbles back at her.

Becky stared.

Something warm and joyous pushed up inside Ivy, and she shared his grin.

Sophia giggled. Then she bounced in his arms.

He pulled her closer, merriment melding into worry once more.

"I believe," Ivy said gently, "she's asking you to do it again."

"Is she?" He tried, and Sophia giggled and bounced some more. Grin returning, he did it once more.

Ivy could only watch them. Sophia's fingers had found his hair, mussing the no-doubt silky strands. His eyes were as bright as his daughter's. Oh, to have them both like this all the time.

To bring him such joy.

After the seventh exchange, he glanced at Ivy. "How long will she continue like this?"

"As long as you are willing," Ivy assured him. "But we could try sitting again, if you'd like."

"No, no." He met Ivy's gaze and sighed, and Sophia's little face bunched as if she felt his frustration. "You are the one I owe an apology, Ivy. You have done so much for Sophia. I just don't want to see her hurt."

"No one who loves a child wants to see that child hurt,"

Ivy told him. "But you have to free her to try new things. It's the only way she'll grow."

He glanced at his daughter, who was reaching for his mustache this time, and held her a little farther away. "But what if she fails?"

"She will fail, at least once," Ivy promised him. "Everyone does. But she must learn to keep trying until she succeeds."

Sophia was wiggling once more, and he bent to set her gently on her rump on the carpet. She glanced around as if surprised to see the world from that angle. But Ivy was pleased to see that she kept her balance.

"Did your father struggle with raising you and your sisters?" Kendall asked, crouching near the baby.

She had to go carefully. She didn't want him to think badly of her father. An injury at the mill and a bad second marriage had driven him into the bottle and an early grave.

"He had to work long hours," Ivy explained. "We didn't see him much. You have the luxury of spending time with Sophia. Remember what you told me? How you wanted to teach her about the stars and clothe her in silk?"

"She's a little young," he temporized, edging to the right as Sophia listed in that direction.

"It's never too early to start," Ivy insisted. "But if you are concerned about her health, perhaps we should have the physician you mentioned visit and let us know his recommendations."

Sophia leaned farther to the right, and Kendall caught her before she hit the carpet. "He comes every other Wednesday and is due tomorrow. I'll be eager to hear his opinion."

So was Ivy. She could only hope this physician was a more reasonable sort, for if he advised coddling Sophia, Ivy and Kendall would be at even greater odds.

CHAPTER TEN

He was being too cautious. Kendall could see it in Ivy's warm brown eyes, hear it in her gentle voice. Worse, he felt it in Sophia's sad cries. How could he explain the sacred duty Adelaide had left him? Sophia was all that remained of his wife. He couldn't risk her, for anything.

And yet, Ivy had already made such a difference in his daughter. Sophia laughed—laughed! As they finished Tuesday and began Wednesday, he realized he had rarely heard his daughter cry. When she cried, Ivy was there to set things right. Sophia's eyes were bright, her movements quick and sure. She had a confidence he had never suspected.

So did Ivy. He had hoped for someone who would put Sophia's needs first, but Ivy's dedication surpassed anything he could have imagined. She was Sophia's champion, and he found it hard to gainsay her. Even when his heart trembled at the things his daughter was attempting under Ivy's watchful eye.

He was prepared for a tongue lashing when Doctor Penrose arrived Wednesday afternoon. Surely the physician would see that they had pushed Sophia too far. Like Kendall, the doctor was following in his father's footsteps. A Doctor Penrose had ushered Kendall's father into the world. The man's son had attended Kendall's mother at both her births, had fought valiantly to save Weston and their mother. Adelaide had insisted on a London physician travelling out for Sophia's birth. The man had stayed a week before their baby was born. And, for all his Edinburgh training and prestigious clientele, he had been unable to save Adelaide.

Kendall shook off the thoughts now as he accompanied Penrose to the new nursery. "Lady Kendall wanted Sophia closer," he explained as he pointed him toward the door.

"Ah, yes, I meant to wish you happy," the doctor said, inclining his head. His light brown hair swept his forehead, and he swiped it aside with one hand as Kendall opened the door to the nursery.

Sophia was on her feet on the rug, bouncing up and down, while Ivy held both hands. Something raced up Kendall, and he dashed into the room. "What are you doing?"

Sophia plopped down on her bottom and began to cry.

Ivy picked her up and straightened, face stern. "You frightened her."

She'd frightened him, but he wasn't about to admit that before the doctor.

"Examine her immediately," he ordered Penrose. "She might have broken something."

Doctor Penrose raised a brow, but he brought his black bag with him into the room and set it on a chair.

"Lady Kendall, allow me to introduce myself," he said with a bow. "Matthias Penrose. I have the honor of being Lady Sophia's physician."

Ivy dipped a curtsey, for all the world as if he outranked her. Sophia's cries ebbed away, and she wiggled in Ivy's arms. Kendall recognized the movement now. She wanted Ivy to bounce up and down again.

"Sir," Ivy said. "A pleasure to meet you. I've heard how important you have been to Lady Sophia's life. Thank you for all you've done."

Was that pink creeping into Penrose's cheeks? The fellow

acted positively smitten.

"I am delighted to be of service," he assured her. He held out his arms. "If I may?"

Ivy surrendered Sophia into his grip and came to stand beside Kendall. He could feel the disapproval radiating off her, and he knew it wasn't the physician who had displeased her.

"Forgive me," he murmured. "I was just surprised."

She nodded but said nothing. Still, her shoulders relaxed just the slightest.

Penrose bounced Sophia up and down in his arms, and she giggled at him. When he stopped, she pressed her legs against his stomach as if urging him to keep going.

He nodded with a smile. "An impressive improvement since I was here last. I estimate she's gained at least a pound. And that rash you were concerned about on her face is gone."

"I believe it may have been caused by excessive crying," Ivy put in.

The physician nodded again. "Quite possible."

"But is she healthy?" Kendall pressed.

"I'll look closer, but I see no reason for concern at the moment," Penrose assured him. "Tell me, what have you done differently?"

Kendall looked to Ivy.

"We started her on solids," she explained. "Mashed vegetables. I thought to try porridge and then fruit next."

"A sensible progression," Doctor Penrose said, moving one finger in front of Sophia's face. Her vivid blue eyes followed it as if wondering what he meant to do next.

"We are providing more things to interest her," Ivy continued. "Taking her on walks about the house and the gardens."

"Sunshine and fresh air have been known to help many an invalid," he noted, stopping his finger under Sophia's lips. She seized it and brought it toward her mouth.

"She has a tooth," Ivy cautioned.

Penrose peered closer. "Indeed she does. That might explain the crying recently. How have you treated it?"

"A silk handkerchief dipped in cold water," Ivy said.

Kendall waited for the dismay his former nurse had expressed. Penrose merely pulled his finger out of Sophia's grip. "Very wise."

He couldn't be so sure. "What if she should swallow it?"

"So long as she is supervised, there is little danger." Penrose took hold of Sophia's arm. Kendall's daughter yanked it back with a frown.

"Improved muscle strength as well, I see," he mused. "Has she crawled yet?"

"No," Ivy admitted. "But she's trying."

His smile widened. "Excellent. All good news." He tugged on each leg in turn, and Sophia began making noises for all the world as if she was scolding him.

He offered her back to Ivy. "Well done, Lady Kendall. You are to be congratulated."

Sophia blew bubbles at him and giggled. He laughed.

Kendall felt as if one of his ceremonial cloaks had been removed from his shoulders, allowing him an easy breath for the first time in a long time. But Ivy was not content.

"Then you see no reason why she may not sit on the carpet, attempt to crawl?" she asked him, turning her body from side to side as if dancing with Sophia.

"None at all," he said. "With supervision, of course. I would not leave her alone in a room."

Kendall raised his head. "Certainly not. She is attended at all times."

"Excellent." He went to pick up his bag, then bowed to Ivy. "Lady Kendall, until next time."

"Sir." Ivy didn't curtsey this time, but her smile said she knew she'd made her case.

Kendall touched her arm. "You were right, I was wrong. Forgive me."

Her smile sent him out of the room with a smile of his own.

He walked his family physician to the door. "I'm glad you approve this approach for Sophia. It is a weight off my mind."

"This is the best course for your daughter," Penrose assured him. "Can't you see the changes in her?"

Kendall nodded. "Of course. I merely questioned the risk."

"Risk of what?" Penrose stopped in the entry hall to eye him. "I heard nothing that said Lady Kendall was doing anything that might harm Lady Sophia."

The doubts were already creeping closer, like thieves intent on stealing his joy. "And the solid food so soon? She has only one tooth. Not much to chew with."

"Not much need to chew," Penrose countered. "Even the elderly and those lacking teeth are given mashes for nourishment. She cannot continue on gruel forever."

There was that. "But is she strong enough for sitting, for crawling?" Kendall pressed. "She might damage her legs and arms permanently."

Penrose peered into his face as if Kendall was the one ailing. "Every baby everywhere attempts to sit, crawl, stand, and eventually walk. These are achievements to celebrate, not prevent."

"I'm not trying to prevent them," Kendall protested. "I just don't want to push her beyond her capability."

"She is far more capable than you know," Penrose assured him, straightening. "And that goes for your new wife as well. I have found many mothers who approach childrearing thoughtfully and logically, and I am encouraged by it. But you have a rare treasure in your wife, my lord. It is clear she dotes on your daughter."

He had always considered Sophia his treasure. He had married Ivy to protect his child. But Penrose was right. Sophia wasn't the only lady in this house who deserved his attentions. It was time he found a way to show Ivy how much he appreciated her.

So, over the next few days, he did his best to fall in line with Ivy's advice concerning Sophia. If he reached for her every time she fell, that was only to be expected. He did not approach Mrs. Grunion about making sure the mash was smooth enough. He did not rearrange the furnishings in the nursery again. He encouraged Ivy and Sophia however he could, even if some part of him whispered he was turning the care of Adelaide's daughter over to someone else.

Perhaps it was his renewed determination, perhaps his praise of Sophia and Ivy, but on Thursday, Ivy brought Sophia to the breakfast room with her. Until then, he and Ivy had taken their breakfasts separately, and Ivy showed no interest in joining him now. His daughter, however, eyed the food before Kendall as if wondering when she might have a taste. He was not ready for her to try eggs and kippered salmon, let alone the hot tea Travis was even now fetching.

"I have a task I must attend to this morning," Ivy announced. "I wonder, would you watch Sophia for a couple of hours?"

"A task?" he asked, standing beside his chair as propriety demanded.

"Yes," she said, and it was clear she had no intention of elaborating. "I could leave her with Becky, but I was under the impression you were less than satisfied with Becky's performance earlier this week."

The nursemaid simply didn't understand what was at stake. Who better to care for his daughter while Ivy was busy than him? Besides, that might assuage some of the guilt he was feeling.

"Very well," he agreed.

"Thank you." Ivy transferred his daughter into his arms. "She has eaten and been changed. She likely won't need a nap until I return. Simply take her with you in whatever you must do. She'll enjoy the change of scenery."

And Ivy left him.

Kendall looked at his daughter. His daughter looked at him. Travis came through the serving door at the back of the room, silver tray in his hands, and actually froze.

"Lady Sophia has breakfasted," Kendall told him, returning to his seat and positioning Sophia on his lap. She reached for the eggs. Kendall pushed back the plate.

The footman set the tea a discreet distance away on the damask draped table.

"Do we have any more of those cinnamon buns we had for tea earlier this week?" Kendall asked him, reaching for his fork. Sophia grabbed a lock of his hair and tugged. He refused to wince.

His head footman's face was its usual impassive mask, though his gaze flickered over the baby in Kendall's lap. "I believe they have been consumed, your lordship, but I will let Mrs. Grunion know you enjoyed them."

He'd enjoyed them immensely. The next hour, however, was challenging. He managed to finish eating with Sophia in his arms, only spilling a bit of the tea on the carpet when she put her finger in his ear. Leaving Travis to clean up the mess, he took his daughter for a walk about the corridors. How wise of his grandfather to make the house into a circle of sorts. He could have wandered for hours. But he did have some work he should attend to. Perhaps a few minutes in his study…

Were not to be expected. As soon as he sat behind his desk, Sophia reached for the quill pen. He moved it out of the way. He caught the ink stand before she could pull it over, wrestled Liverpool's bills out of her grip before she could do more than leave a damp thumbprint, and pushed the sanding box to the other side of the polished walnut surface.

Sophia pouted.

"My lord," Travis said from the doorway.

Kendall looked up, some part of him reaching as eagerly for relief. "Yes. Is Ivy looking for Sophia?"

"Not to my knowledge, my lord," his footman said in his usual confident tone, gaze in the distance as if he hadn't noticed the squirming mass of child in Kendall's lap. "Sir Alexander has arrived from London. On a matter of some urgency, I gather. May I show him in?"

"Certainly," Kendall said, leaning back in the chair behind his desk to keep Sophia from launching herself onto the surface. "And inform Mrs. Sheppard to see about a room for him tonight."

"I believe he wishes to return to the City today, my lord." Travis stepped closer and lowered his voice. "Would you like me to see to her ladyship while you converse?"

For a moment he thought his man meant Ivy, then he realized he was asking about Sophia. Kendall rose and hefted his daughter higher in his arms. "Thank you, Travis, but I believe myself capable of entertaining her ladyship for a while longer."

Travis inclined his head, but that stiff back spoke of endless doubts. He returned immediately with the family's solicitor.

Sir Alexander had served Kendall's father faithfully and had continued in his role as legal advisor when Kendall had come into the title. He had been away serving the King of late, but his firm had continued managing Kendall's affairs during that time. He strode into the room with considerable energy, black coattails rustling, and he only faltered a moment as his gaze fell on the baby in Kendall's arms.

Sophia shrank closer to Kendall.

"Good morning, Alex," he greeted him. "May I make you known to a particularly fine young lady?"

Alex ventured closer, as if not at all sure Sophia wouldn't bite. "I would be honored."

Kendall looked down at his daughter, who gazed up at him, blue eyes unblinking. "Sophia, this is Sir Alexander. You can trust him with all your secrets."

Sophia blew bubbles.

As she laughed, Alex recoiled. "Where did she learn that?"

"She discovered it all on her own," Kendall said, feeling an absurd sense of pride in the fact. "Ivy says it will be some time before she tires of it."

"Ah, the new Lady Kendall," his solicitor said, straightening. "I heard congratulations were in order."

Kendall nodded him into one of the leather-bound chairs on that side of the desk and went to take the other, making Sophia comfortable in his lap. She set about examining the buttons on his paisley waistcoat. "Thank you, and welcome back."

The solicitor inclined his head. "It seems there have been quite a few changes while I was away."

"Nothing vital, that I recall," Kendall said. "I did little with our investments. I've been too busy with other matters to even review your staff's work."

Alex's eyes glittered. "So I was informed. Tell me about your bride. Another love match, I gather."

The chair felt harder than he remembered. He'd have to see about replacing it. "Lady Kendall and I are reasonably happy." He shifted Sophia as she tried to bring one of his buttons to her mouth.

"And you have cause to be," Alex assured him. "A very presentable young woman, I hear. She must be delighted to have garnered such a catch, not an easy feat from her position."

Kendall stiffened, and Sophia looked up at him with a frown. "She is the sister of a baronet."

"Sister to the Beast of Birmingham," Alex corrected him with a tut. "I heard distressing rumors about that family's ability to crawl up into Society."

Kendall kept his face polite from long practice. "Ivy Bateman did not marry me to further herself. I had to beg her to accept my proposal."

Sophia seemed to sense the annoyance in his tone, for her little face began to pucker. He bounced her gently on his knee, and her smile returned. Would that he could find his calm so easily.

"And yet, the gossips have it she allowed herself to be compromised."

Kendall opened his mouth, and Alex waved a hand. "You need not deny it. You are the talk of London. And I am kept informed by the Runner who investigated matters for your father."

Kendall frowned. "I requested no investigation."

Alex inclined his head. "That is my role as your man of affairs. My apologies if my staff overstepped themselves in my absence. I was not pleased with them for failing to draw up the marriage arrangements to protect you, though it sounds as if we need not worry your new bride will spend every penny of your inheritance, given your faith in her."

Kendall realized his leg was jiggling Sophia up and down perhaps more vigorously than was wise and slowed its pace. "I assure you, you will have no suspicions once you meet her. I know I have encouraged you in plain speaking, Alex, and I thank you for your concern, but Ivy poses no danger to me."

His solicitor leaned back in his chair. "Then she won't mind signing the agreements after the fact."

"Not at all," Kendall said, switching Sophia to his other knee. "Draw up what you think best. Just ensure that it includes a generous dower settlement for Ivy and decent dowries for her sisters Miss Daisy Bateman and Miss Petunia Bateman."

Alex's firm jaw looked harder than the chair. "Then she's already won concessions from you."

"On the contrary. I offered the terms to her." Sophia

caught his button, and he twisted to prevent her from biting it. He would have to talk to Ivy about this fascination.

Alex was no less fixated. "It wasn't enough you were making her a marchioness?"

Denied her prize, Sophia turned in his arms and blew bubbles at Alex again. He looked no more pleased by the second attempt than he had the first.

Kendall stood, lifting Sophia higher against his shoulder. "Have a care, Alex. My wife deserves nothing but respect from you."

Alex held up both hands. "I mean no disrespect. But as your solicitor, it is my duty to counsel you on financial matters. And as a friend, I feel it my duty to counsel you on matters of the heart."

"This isn't a matter of the heart," Kendall told him. "Ivy and I have an agreement. She has already more than surpassed her side. I intend to do no less."

"Very well," Alex said, lowering his hands. "Just be careful. I would not want you to allow this woman into your home, into your daughter's life, only to regret it."

CHAPTER ELEVEN

Ivy left her apron in the kitchen and started for the door. Still a half hour before she must accept Sophia back from Kendall. She was highly tempted to take a quick nap. She hadn't cared for a baby in nearly ten years. She'd forgotten how exhausting it could be.

And how exhilarating.

Sophia had stopped crying for the most part. She regarded the world with bright eyes. And not only could she sit on her own, but she'd tried to crawl. Amazing! Ivy could hardly wait to see what tomorrow brought.

She hadn't expected today to bring trouble.

She found Kendall and Sophia in his study, an unlikely place for a baby he'd refused to allow in the library. She was further surprised to spot another man with them. He was heavily built, with black hair and well-tailored clothing nearly as dark. He climbed to his feet at the sight of Ivy, as did Kendall. Sophia waved her arms in greeting.

"Ivy, allow me to introduce Sir Alexander Prentice, our solicitor," Kendall said.

The older man swept her a bow. "Lady Kendall. A pleasure. I've heard a great deal about you."

Normally the phrase suggested praise, but there was something about the way he said it that made Ivy wish she'd worn a better dress than her blue cambric today. As she moved closer, she saw Kendall's smile waiver as his gaze brushed her cheek. Her hand reached up to touch her face and came away white with flour.

"I seem to have misplaced my puff," she said brightly, brushing the telltale signs away and hoping none speckled her gown or Percy would sigh in vexation. "Powder can be so time-consuming."

Both men smiled politely. Sophia blew bubbles at her.

"I wonder, your lordship," the solicitor said smoothly, "if perhaps Lady Sophia could be surrendered to her nurse so that I might discuss matters with Lady Kendall."

Kendall lifted Sophia higher. "Either Ivy or I attend to Lady Sophia's needs. If we are both needed, she stays."

Ivy beamed at him.

Sophia screwed up her face, cheeks turning red.

Kendall's smile faded into alarm. "What's wrong with her?"

Ivy came to take her from his grip, feeling the warmth against her arm. "Lady Sophia requires a change."

Kendall looked positively horrified.

His solicitor's face wrinkled, like Sophia when she had tried the peas. "As I said, perhaps it is time to call for her nurse."

Kendall squared his shoulders. "No need. I will take her to Becky. I'll return shortly." He accepted his daughter back from Ivy with only the faintest of flinches at the scent wafting up and bore her from the room.

"I see you and Lord Kendall have worked out an arrangement," the solicitor said in the silence that followed.

Did he know theirs was a marriage of convenience? Ivy merely smiled, dropping her gaze as she went to sit opposite the man.

"I have seldom seen his lordship so besotted," the solicitor said.

He wasn't besotted in the slightest, but if Kendall had given that impression to his man of affairs, she would not attempt to change it. She met his gaze and was surprised to find his look calculating.

"What did you wish to discuss, Sir Alexander?" she asked.

He leaned back and clasped his hands over one knee. "Straight to the point. Always my preference. Lord Kendall neglected to have me draw up the necessary papers for your dower arrangement. I will bring them to you to sign within a week's time. I'll make sure you have the use of the dower house as long as you live and suitable funds to support yourself."

Ivy waited, but he did not continue. Indeed, he was smiling amicably as if he'd granted her a boon she could not possibly deserve.

"And dowries for my two sisters," she said.

His smile broadened. Why did it feel as if he had patted her on the head? "I know a gentleman promises many things while courting. If you had come to me, I could have explained that such gifts are not necessary when a lady has a brother who should be responsible."

But what a burden to put on Matty, especially now that he'd married Charlotte. The money they saved should go to their own children one day.

"I did not realize it was an unusual arrangement," Ivy said. "Lord Kendall offered it, and I accepted. I would expect him to honor his word."

"And it is my duty to prevent him from overexerting himself."

Overexerting? Was the estate mortgaged? She glanced around at all the gilding and marble. Had his forebears squandered their money to build such a palace, to protect that Roman pavement?

Ivy squared her shoulders. "I will economize if it means providing for my sisters. I can cook and clean. I need no fancy dresses or jewels."

He stared at her. Then he barked a laugh and wagged a finger at her. "Ah, I can see you will have your little joke, but I must insist. Lord Kendall had no business offering you such a fortune. You brought nothing to this marriage. You received a gracious home, more pin money than you could possibly spend."

She had brought far more than that, but Ivy seized on two of his words. "Pin money? How much pin money?"

He paused, then cautiously named a sum as if he expected her to bargain over the amount. It was more than Matty had made as a bodyguard in a year.

"A month?" she pressed.

"Yes," he allowed, frown gathering on his dark brow.

She calculated quickly. If she kept her expenses to her usual amount, she'd have a fine dowry for Daisy in two years' time. Think what she could save for Tuny and Sophia.

Ivy smiled at him. "Then I will be delighted to sign your papers, sir. Thank you for explaining things to me."

For some reason, his charming smile looked strained as he pushed to his feet. "Always glad to be able to assist Lord Kendall. Good day, madam."

He left the room, and Mrs. Sheppard glided in. Surely she hadn't been listening outside the door. Ivy felt her cheeks heating nonetheless.

"Where did you wish tea to be served this afternoon, your ladyship?" the housekeeper asked.

Ivy nearly asked for a cup in her room as she had taken it the last two days, but an idea beckoned. "Where does Lord Kendall generally take tea?"

"In the emerald salon, your ladyship, at precisely three."

It was nearly that now. "Then I will take it with him after he has bid farewell to Sir Alexander. That will make less work for you."

Mrs. Sheppard nodded, started to turn away, then paused and looked back. "You do realize, Lady Kendall, that we serve you, and not the other way around. You have no need to tailor your life for our convenience."

She'd always been the one to cook and clean at home, first for her ailing mother, then her spiteful stepmother.

NEVER MARRY A MARQUESS 109

Even though she'd set her sisters chores, the responsibility had fallen to her, especially after they'd moved to London and she'd begun caring for Matthew's home. She knew how hard it could be. She wasn't about to increase the burden on others.

And if the estate was struggling, all the more reason not to add to the staff's woes. Small wonder Mrs. Sheppard had feared Ivy might discharge some of the staff. It must cost a fortune to house and feed all these people, let alone pay them their quarterly wages.

But the housekeeper might not know how tenuous their standing. Ivy certainly didn't want to be the one to tell her.

"Do unto others," she said to Mrs. Sheppard. "My mother insisted on it, and I have made it my habit as well. So, today, I will take tea with his lordship, as a wife should. Please have Becky find me if Sophia needs me in any way."

The housekeeper agreed, and Ivy went to the emerald salon.

The room was empty as she entered, so she had a moment to wander past the patterned silk wall hangings that had given the room its name. She seemed to recall Mrs. Bateman turning down similar material once as being too costly. Here it covered from the ivory wainscoting to the gilded cornices of the high ceiling, except where the white marble fireplace and wide windows overlooking the drive interrupted the expanse of green. All the furnishings were gilded too. If they needed money, she could see doing without half of the dozen chairs sprinkled about the room and perhaps those massive gold urns between the emerald-draped windows.

And who was she to make such arrangements, even in her mind? Only when Charlotte had come into their lives had their sitting room furnishings looked even half as fancy. If Ivy hadn't married Kendall, she might well have been the one scrubbing the floors or shining the windows, not sitting on the grand sofa before the marble hearth as if she was a lady to the manor born.

Still, she sat a little taller as Kendall appeared in the doorway.

From the moment she'd met him, at a ball hosted by the Countess of Carrolton more than a month ago, she'd been awed at the elegance of him. Even now, after tending to Sophia for more than two hours, he was calm, in control. Not even a hair of his mustache was out of place as he walked toward Ivy and offered her a bow. His poise had its appeal, even if she had never lived a life that would allow such perfection.

"Do I take it you'll be joining me for tea?" he asked, straightening.

"Sophia is cared for, so yes, if it pleases you," Ivy replied.

He flipped up his coattails to sit beside her. "It pleases me a great deal. Thank you for suggesting I spend time with Sophia this morning. I begin to see the challenge I've given you."

"She is a darling," Ivy assured him.

The mother-of-pearl-faced clock on the gilded mantel chimed three.

Mrs. Sheppard moved into the room with a footman who was wheeling a tea cart. The fine china cups patterned in blue and copper like the Roman pavement chimed as he positioned the cart near Ivy and withdrew to stand by the doorway in case he was needed. The teapot was silver—of course—and so polished she could see her reflection in it.

That would fetch a pretty penny, if they needed it.

Mrs. Sheppard curtsied to Ivy. "Shall I pour, your ladyship?"

Ivy had usually poured for Matthew and her sisters. But she didn't want to disrupt Kendall's routine any more than necessary. "Yes, thank you."

The housekeeper dispensed the brew. Ivy watched her. She served Kendall first, a full cup of the rich amber tea, no sugar, lemon, or milk.

"How do you prefer your tea, your ladyship?" she asked.

"The same," Ivy said.

Kendall smiled, but he waited until she had been served to take a sip. Ivy blew away the steam before bringing the cup to her mouth. As the tea touched her tongue, she drew back with a frown.

Mrs. Sheppard must have been watching her too. "Something amiss?" she asked.

Kendall glanced at Ivy as well.

It was wretched tea, bitter and speckled with leaves. Matthew had had better, on his limited income. Couldn't they afford to do the same? She almost protested, then erased the frown from her face. She should not complain if this was the best the housekeeper had to offer.

"I just wasn't expecting this variety," Ivy explained. "Is this what you prefer, my lord?"

Mrs. Sheppard transferred her gaze to Kendall.

"I have become accustomed to it," he said.

So, someone else had introduced it to the house. His late wife, perhaps? That would explain the red rising above his beard. She made a note to discuss the matter with the housekeeper.

"Would you serve the biscuits, Mrs. Sheppard?" Ivy asked. She certainly needed one if she was to get through this cup.

Now Kendall frowned. "Biscuits?"

Mrs. Sheppard's hand froze in the act of reaching for the snowy platter on the tea tray. "Yes, my lord. Lady Kendall's choice."

His brow cleared, and he selected one of the thin Naples biscuits from the platter. Ivy accepted one as well, but she waited for him to take a bite, heart starting to beat faster.

He bit into the crisp rosewater-flavored biscuit. His brow went up. He took another bite and finished the biscuit with the third. "That was very good. I'll take another."

Beaming, Mrs. Sheppard extended the platter again.

Crumbs clung to his mustache—creamy white against the sable. Ivy hugged her cup close to keep from reaching out and brushing them away from his lips. He ate through a second and a third biscuit, tea forgotten.

"In my family," Ivy ventured, "we often dip them in the tea, like this." She suited word to action, then brought the dripping sweet to her lips.

Just in time to see Mrs. Sheppard's eyes widen in shock.

Apparently, marchionesses didn't dunk their biscuits in their tea.

Yet Kendall was willing to try. He cautiously inserted his biscuit into the cup, then brought it out and took a bite. "Interesting," he said after swallowing. He finished the biscuit, then sipped at his tea. "And it improves the taste of the brew as well."

Ivy relaxed against the sofa.

But not for long. Kendall set aside his tea and reached to take the platter of biscuits from the housekeeper's grip and position it on the table in front of him, as if intending to finish the batch himself. "These are marvelous. My compliments to Mrs. Grunion. An experiment, I take it?"

Mrs. Sheppard busied herself straightening the teapot. "Yes, my lord."

"Then it is a smashing success," he said. "I don't ever recall anyone baking like this before."

Mrs. Sheppard met Ivy's gaze, and for a moment Ivy thought the housekeeper would tell him the truth of the biscuits' origin. But she merely turned to Kendall with a smile. "We have a new baker. She is quite talented."

Ivy's cheeks felt as warm as her heart.

Kendall picked up his cup again. "A new baker, eh? What do you think, Ivy? Is there something you've craved?"

A kiss from you?

Goodness, where had that thought come from? There would be no kisses shared between them. She'd known that when she'd married him.

"These are among my favorites," she confessed. "But what of you, my lord? Did you have no treat that thrilled you as a boy?"

He pursed his lips as if considering the matter. They were a soft rose, in keeping with his dark coloring. She could lean forward, capture his lips with her own.

Why did she persist in thinking of kisses!

"I seem to recall an overindulgence in anise biscuits," Mrs. Sheppard put in.

He laughed. "Oh, yes. Right before Eton. Father wasn't pleased when he discovered a full dozen missing." He turned to Ivy. "They were his favorite too, you see. We had quite a discussion on the importance of putting the needs of others before your own."

And his father's words had obviously made an impression. He had even pledged his life to a near stranger so Sophia could have a mother.

"Would it be possible to procure some anise seed, Mrs. Sheppard?" Ivy asked.

The housekeeper smiled. "I'm certain it can be arranged, your ladyship. I'll be sure to alert our baker as soon as they arrive." She curtsied and left them then.

Kendall leaned back, cradling his cup in his hands. "Do you know, I never thought about the tea before. It's rather wretched."

Ivy bit back a laugh. "It is. Would you like me to see about something better?"

He hesitated, then set his cup on the table. "Yes, thank you."

Now Ivy hesitated. "If there's an issue of cost…"

He waved a hand. "Whatever you like. Mrs. Sheppard can see that it's ordered the next time we send to London for meat."

Ivy eyed him. "You send all the way to London for meat? Isn't that expensive?"

He turned and took her hand in his own. "Ivy, you

needn't worry about cost. Look around you. I would spare
no expense to make you and Sophia happy."

Perhaps, but might that have been the thing that had
caused the estate to struggle? Still, she knew a man's pride.
Her father had refused to discuss money with his daughters,
to the point that she had had no idea what he had left
them when he had died. Mrs. Bateman had claimed they
were penniless and lucky that she was willing to allow
them to keep living in their home, which she now owned.
Matthew had been similarly tight-lipped about his income,
though he had given her a specific budget in which she
had to confine her spending for the house.

And she had pin money. She would use it to help Kendall,
the staff, and her sisters.

Kendall rose beside her and glanced out the window.
"Lovely afternoon for a stroll. Would you be interested in
joining me, Ivy? We can have a footman run out if Sophia
needs you."

A walk on his arm, sunlight bathing his face, gleaming in
his dark eyes. What more could she want?

"I'd be delighted, my lord," she said.

CHAPTER TWELVE

Meredith smiled at the pile of responses on the secretary before her. Something soft and feathery, most likely a tail, brushed her ankle below her lavender skirts, and she glanced down. Fortune was eyeing the open desk.

"You know very well it won't bear your weight," Meredith reminded her pet. "We've already repaired it twice since I purchased it six months ago." She shifted to block the cat from making a third attempt.

Fortune leaped up on her lap instead and raised her head over the edge of the drop-down desk as if covertly studying the enemy. One white-tipped paw reached up to bat at the paper there. Meredith caught the parchment before it could fall.

"Show some respect, if you please," she told her pet. "These are all notes from friends assuring us they will attend the wedding."

Fortune regarded the pile, head cocked and ear twitching, as if listening to voices from the notes.

Truly, the response was gratifying. Nearly everyone she and Julian had invited had replied that they would attend—clever Yvette and her love, the earl of Carrolton, the always energetic Lydia and Lord Worthington, and savvy Charlotte and her pugilist husband, Sir Matthew, along with Miss Bateman and her sister Petunia.

"Alas, Rufus has not responded," Meredith told Fortune.

Fortune pouted.

There were others. Julian had invited colleagues and acquaintances such as the Marquis of Hastings and his son Lord Petersborough. Since it was a wedding, perhaps the old codger would forego attempting to draw Julian into his web of aristocratic intelligence agents. She had plans for her husband—plans to love and cherish him, plans to spend a good part of every day together, making up for the time they'd lost. And perhaps, one day, a family.

Only three invitations had yet to receive a response. One was to Ivy and Lord Kendall, who may have been too busy settling into their new life to manage it. Meredith intended to check in on them at the wedding. Though she hadn't placed Ivy into her position, she felt some responsibility. Still, if Ivy was unhappy, Meredith had no mechanism to remove her.

The second invitation she hoped would come back with a negative reply. She really didn't want Sir Alex at her wedding. She had heard he had returned to England, but Julian had only mentioned that he had seen his mentor. She had been the one to extend the invitation, for Julian's sake.

"And here is one from dear Patience," Meredith said, running a thumb under the wax to break the seal. The pretty companion had been her second client, after Jane, and Meredith and Fortune had spent a particularly memorable if utterly dismal house party over Easter with Patience, her now-husband, Sir Harold Orwell, and his aunt Augusta, a celebrated apothecary.

The invitation had been accepted, as she had hoped, but Patience's note accompanying her acceptance made Meredith sit taller in her seat.

Meredith, a fellow was by the other day. He started at the back door, talking with the staff. As you might expect, when Cuddlestone realized he was after gossip, our dear butler sent him packing. But he returned the next day requesting to speak to Harry. I'm quite pleased to report my husband chased him off the property. The local watch has been alerted, as have Harry's more colorful friends in the village, so I do not expect a return engagement. However, I thought you should be warned. He asked a number of questions as to how I happened to arrive at Foulness Manor, what they thought of you as the instigator, and, most concerning, what Harry might have left me in his will! I almost wish Harry hadn't been his usual impetuous self, for I might have been able to discover who set this miscreant on your tail. Do take care, my dear.

Meredith lowered the note, and Fortune smacked it off the table, then jumped down in pursuit of it. Why would someone assume there was something nefarious in Sir Harry's will? Patience's baronet husband had been known to try his hand at spying for the Crown, using the local smugglers to travel to France and back, but that had nothing to do with Patience or Meredith for that matter.

So, who could be searching for secrets, and why?

Kendall always enjoyed walking about the estate. The ground sloped down around the house in all directions. His father had claimed a man might see tomorrow if he tried hard enough. For the moment, he was content with today.

He wasn't sure what had prompted him to invite Ivy. Adelaide had ever refused the offer, teasing him that he must be a farmer at heart that he enjoyed being out in the fields so much.

"If I cannot drive to it, why would I want to go?" she'd asked him with a laugh.

Yet here was Ivy, matching his steps, heedless of the wheat kernels dotting the skirts of her blue gown, the sun turning her hair to gold.

"I should have given you time to fetch a bonnet," he realized.

Ivy shrugged, fingers skimming the heads of the grain. "It's not so bright I need one."

"How brave of you," he said with a smile. "I know ladies who refuse to set one foot out of doors without covering their skin. Freckles appear to be a curse."

Her hand flew to her nose. "Will I shame you?"

He made a show of stopping in the field. "What, madam, have you been hiding this secret? Let me see the extent of this dire pox." He bent closer. Her skin was creamy, smooth, and beginning to turn the faintest of pinks. Without thinking, he reached up a hand and touched the soft of her cheek. "No freckles, but I wouldn't worry. Freckles on you would look like cinnamon on a biscuit. Absolutely delightful."

He could lose himself in the wonder of her gaze. "I think you're teasing me."

He made himself straighten. "Only a little. It is a lovely day. You should be safe for a time."

She lowered her hand and tilted back her chin, exposing the length of her throat. "Oh, good. You're right. It's far too lovely to hide under a bonnet."

She certainly was.

He shoved away the guilt that threatened. There was no shame in admiring beauty, so long as he did not covet it for his own.

He paused and pointed to the trees ahead of them. "There runs the River Blackmole, a placid stream where trout congregate. You would not know it, but spring frequently pushes it beyond its banks as far as we are standing now."

She glanced around as if trying to imagine the grain covered by a glassy sea. "Has it ever reached the house?"

"Only once, before I was born. Every river flooded that year, I'm told. Villa Romanesque was surrounded, the waters lapping at the base of the stairs. It even trickled over the pavement, until my father packed the edges with burlap bags filled with sand. I could tell it gave him quite a scare."

"You and your father were close," she said, gaze returning to his.

Kendall smiled. "He was my teacher, my mentor, my friend. I miss him keenly."

She touched his hand, her fingers warm. "Matthew took that role for me. He has always been my rock, my shelter."

That was his role now.

The fact seized him. Theirs was a marriage of convenience, but everyone needed someone they could count on. He must be that person for Ivy.

"I will always protect you, Ivy," he murmured.

She wrapped her fingers around his, as if attaching herself to his side. "You are a born protector, I see that. But sometimes, those who are being protected want more."

He thought she meant Sophia, but her gaze was as warm as her fingers. He was leaning closer before he thought better of it.

Suddenly her gaze veered past his shoulder toward the drive. Turning, he spied a lone rider coming in fast.

"Who could that be?" he wondered aloud.

Ivy stepped closer. "My brother. Something must be wrong."

Hands still clasped, they waded through the grain to meet him on the drive.

The sight of Sir Matthew standing on the gravel, feet planted in the stance of a pugilist, set every one of Kendall's nerves alight. Before his elevation for saving the prince's life, Ivy's brother had been known as the Beast of Birmingham. His prowess in the boxing square would have given any sane man pause before facing him. Now his brown coat and breeches were dusty from the road, his short-cropped brown hair stuck out here and there from the ride, and there was a decided set to his rugged face.

"What do you have to say for yourselves?" he demanded as Kendall and Ivy approached.

One of the grooms had come up to take the horse but waited with obvious hesitation to interfere. Kendall gave him a nod of encouragement as Ivy turned to her brother.

"Good afternoon to you too, Matthew," she said with her usual grace. "Would you care for some refreshment after your ride? There are Naples biscuits."

Her brother's scowl didn't ease. "Did he force you into this?"

Kendall would not allow Ivy to be berated. He raised his head and took a step closer to her. "I proposed to your sister, and she accepted. That should be good enough for any man."

Sir Matthew opened his mouth, and Ivy closed the distance to lay a hand on his burley arm. "Please, Matty. Come inside. We can discuss this civilly." Her gaze drifted to the waiting groom.

Sir Matthew followed her gaze, then his face swung forward, and he snapped a nod. Kendall waved to the groom to take the horse. Then he led Ivy and her brother into the house.

Travis was on duty in the entry hall, but he stiffened when he saw Sir Matthew. Ivy's brother had come with no hat or overcoat. In all his travel dust, he looked like nothing as much as a farm hand who had wandered through the wrong door. Travis glanced to Kendall, as if for guidance.

"Sir Matthew Bateman," Kendall informed him, "has come to see his sister."

Travis bowed smoothly. "Would Sir Matthew like to refresh himself after his travels, my lord?"

The former pugilist frowned as if he didn't much like being discussed in the third person, and the scowl was enough to set Travis back a step. "He would not."

Still Travis addressed himself to Kendall. "And will he require a room for the night?"

"Depends on how this discussion goes," Sir Matthew drawled.

Ivy had evidently had enough. "Come this way, Matty," she said, and Kendall and her brother followed her to the emerald salon.

The baronet glanced around the room as they entered. "At least you put her up in nice surroundings."

"It's not like that, Matty," Ivy started, but he held up a hand.

"You offered refreshment. Tea and biscuits would be very welcome after a long ride."

She glanced at Kendall, then back at her brother. "Perhaps not tea, but lemonade. Excuse me a moment while I tell Mrs. Sheppard, the housekeeper." She slipped from the room before Kendall could remind her they had only to ring.

As soon as she was out of earshot, Sir Matthew narrowed his eyes at Kendall. "Care to explain why you rushed her to the altar behind my back?"

He refused to cringe. "I regret we couldn't delay the wedding. I was urgently needed at home."

Ivy's brother crossed his arms over his chest, straining the seams on his coat. "So, why didn't you go home, fix the problem, and then return for Ivy?"

Kendall shifted on the carpet. "It wasn't so easy as that. But, as I said, your sister accepted my proposal. I promise you I will care for her."

Sir Matthew eyed him as if he didn't believe a word of it. "Do you have sisters?"

"No," Kendall admitted, blinking at the *non sequitur*. "A brother."

"Then you can't understand," Matthew said. "I'm the eldest. Our father ceased his ability to care when Ivy was five and I was eleven. *I've* been her father since then. I provided for her, protected her. I want to be sure of the man who thinks he can fill that role for her now."

Kendall spread his hands. "As you can see, I am well equipped to provide."

"And to protect?" Matthew challenged.

Something welled up inside him, surprising him by its strength. "Ivy is my wife. I would lay down my life for her."

Sir Matthew dropped his arms "Then we may not need to have words after all."

His breath left him in a rush, as if it was just as glad to have escaped the fury of Sir Matthew's fists. Still, Kendall managed to seat himself without appearing to fall onto the sofa. Sir Matthew deigned to sit in a chair nearby.

Mrs. Sheppard appeared then with a tea tray. Ivy was right behind her, Sophia in her arms. Kendall stood until she had seated herself beside him. His daughter regarded Sir Matthew with solemn eyes.

"Who's this, then?" he growled.

Kendall bristled, but, instead of taking fright at the rough sound, Sophia giggled. Kendall stared at her in wonder.

"This is Lady Sophia," Ivy said with a fond look at his daughter. "Lord Kendall was concerned for her health, and I wanted to help him nurse her. So, we hurried our wedding for her sake. I left you a note explaining all this. Didn't you notice it on the secretary in your study?"

That scowl could surely curdle milk. "There was no letter on my secretary."

Ivy sighed. "I expect it was mislaid. Please ask Daisy about the matter."

The look they shared spoke volumes. Ivy's younger sister was certainly a bold one and not above speaking her mind in public. But why would she purposefully withhold the letter explaining their marriage?

From the safety of Ivy's lap, Sophia blew bubbles.

Sir Matthew's gaze veered to the baby, and Kendall had to grip the arm of the sofa to keep from snatching his daughter away from the sharp gaze. "What's that you said?" Ivy's brother demanded.

Sophia giggled again.

"Oh, find me funny, do you?" To Kendall's astonishment, Sir Matthew dropped off the chair onto all fours and advanced on the baby, growling like a bear. Sophia clapped her hands, then reached out and snagged a lock of his hair.

Sir Matthew collapsed on the rug. "Ow! Ow! Ow! You've slain me."

Sophia laughed and laughed.

The sound tugged at Kendall's heart, pulling him closer. Why had he never brought such joy to his precious child?

"Do get up, Matty," Ivy said, smiling. "Your lemonade is waiting."

Mrs. Sheppard, who had managed to pour three glasses, shook herself from her reverie. "Biscuit, Sir Matthew?"

"Don't mind if I do," he said, righting himself and returning to his seat with easy grace.

"Set the plate in front of Lord Kendall when you're finished, Mrs. Sheppard," Ivy instructed.

Already she knew him. Kendall accepted the glass and gazed at his bride over the rim. Her color was high, her eyes sparkled. She caught his gaze on her and smiled, and warmth pushed up into the part of him that had been frozen since Adelaide's death.

He focused his gaze on the pale-yellow liquid in his glass. He had loved Adelaide. He would love her forever. Could he truly make room in his heart for another?

CHAPTER THIRTEEN

Ivy played with Sophia's hands as she, her brother, and Kendall debated the need for formal regulations on the sport of pugilism. She would not have doubted Matthew's interest in the topic. She was only surprised by her husband's passion on the subject.

"A boxing match pits skill against skill," he insisted, setting aside his glass and leaning forward. "In the heat of the moment, it's all too easy to lose your head, do more harm than you intended."

He certainly would never lose his head. He held his emotions too tightly. Did he know how Matthew had come to be called the Beast?

It was a sign that he had left the Beast behind that her brother merely nodded. "That's true enough. But if the man has no honor, regulations won't stop him from doing his worst."

"A rule can only be enforced once it's been broken," Ivy agreed.

"But it can be enforced," Kendall countered. "A fellow might be sanctioned, barred from entering the square again. Surely that would offer some protection."

Protection again. Did the man never take a risk?

"Some," Matthew allowed. He paused to reach for another of the Naples biscuits. "I see you haven't lost your touch, Ivy."

Kendall glanced her way, and she clutched Sophia closer with the odd notion she could hide behind her.

"Yes, our baker is quite skilled," she said hastily, cheeks heating. "I'll be sure to pass along your compliments."

Her brother cast her a look out of the corner of his eyes, but he said no more before he popped the biscuit whole into his mouth.

"You will stay with us tonight, Sir Matthew," Kendall said. "It's too late in the day to start back for London now."

Ivy thought Matthew might stiffen at the lordly tone, but he merely nodded. "I'd be glad for the bed and board. And more time with this little sweetie." He lowered his head and growled at Sophia. The baby had been eyeing Ivy's glass of lemonade on the table before them ever since Mrs. Sheppard had left, as if determining how she might manage a sip. Now she reached out a hand toward Matthew, and he pulled back before she could clasp his hair again.

Ivy smiled. She'd nearly forgotten about the Great Bear. Matthew had played the game with Daisy and Tuny when they were little. Likely he'd played it with her as well, but she had been acting as mother for so long she didn't remember being a child most days. Though Sophia was no blood relative, marriage made him her uncle. Ivy was willing to allow the family to expand, even if Kendall wasn't.

"Sophia likely requires a nap," Kendall said.

Ivy glanced down at the little girl in her arms, who showed not the least sign of being tired. Indeed, her blue eyes moved from her father to her uncle and back again, as if she wondered who would be the first to play with her.

"She would benefit from something that tired her," Ivy said. "Perhaps we could show Matthew the pavement."

Kendall brightened, but her brother frowned. "The pavement? Are you throwing me out?"

"Not at all," Kendall said, rising. "It's a feature of Villa

Romanesque, and a treasure of my family. I'd be delighted to show it to you."

Ivy lifted Sophia higher, and they all left the room.

She caught her brother eyeing the house as they crossed through the entry hall and into the opposite corridor.

"They certainly like marble," he murmured to her.

"Wait till you see the pavement room," she warned him.

Her brother was suitably amazed. He wandered past the statues, pausing to examine each one. "Fine work here," he told Kendall.

"Not originals, for the most part," Kendall said, "but patterned after the Greek or Roman period. Father disagreed with Lord Elgin's appropriation of the Parthenon friezes."

Matthew stuck out his lower lip as if impressed.

But he stood over the pavement and stared.

"Never saw anything like it," he finally said after Kendall had explained its history. "Nearly fifteen hundred years old, you say?"

"Not a day younger," Kendall assured him.

Matthew shook his head.

Head high with pride, Kendall slipped his arm about Ivy's waist.

She managed not to drop Sophia onto the pavement, but it was a near-run thing. She was afraid even to breathe lest Kendall realize what he was doing and stop. The way he held her, as if it were the two of them and Sophia united, was more amazing than the pavement at her feet. She nearly cried out when he pulled back to escort Matthew from the room.

"We'll dine at six," Kendall said as they headed toward the entry hall. "A footman can show you the way to the dining room. I don't plan to change."

Matthew laughed, catching Sophia's attention and earning a smile. "I couldn't change if I wanted to. I didn't bring a bag."

Kendall's brows went up, and he looked her brother up and down. "I'd offer you a coat, but it would hardly fit. And I'm not sure what to do about a nightshirt."

Only one man in the house might be large enough to have clothes that would fit her brother's frame. After seeing her brother to his room and settling Sophia in the nursery, Ivy went in search of Travis.

The footman's blond brows tweaked just the slightest when she explained the situation, but he promised to take care of the matter. He and her brother were standing outside the guest room door when she came out of her room a short while later, blue cotton nightshirt in her brother's hands.

"And my thanks for it," he was telling the footman. "Were you a boxer?"

"No, Sir Matthew," he replied, but the look on his face said he was pleased Matthew had suggested otherwise.

Dinner was a fine affair. She had become accustomed to the rich dishes, but her brother did the salmon in dill sauce justice. And Kendall's glances to her only made the food taste sweeter.

"Allow me to send you off in the morning," Kendall said as the three of them climbed the stairs for bed.

Matthew nodded agreeably. Then Kendall turned for the right, and Ivy led Matthew to the left.

"Nice of you to walk me to my room," her brother said. "Fellow could get lost in this pile."

"It's actually very well laid out," Ivy said, pausing before her door. "My room is just down from yours, should you need anything in the night."

He frowned, glancing back the way Kendall had gone. "You and his lordship don't share a room?"

She could not have this conversation with her brother. "I wanted a suite so I could be close to Sophia."

His frown turned to her. "Sophia is his daughter. Shouldn't he be close as well?"

"I hope he will be, in time. Sophia is all he has left of his first wife, Matty. Sometimes I think he's afraid to so much as touch her lest he lose her too."

His frown eased. "So, he makes you his nanny."

"No," Ivy corrected him. "I'm not Sophia's nanny. I'm her mother. I promise you, the role is no imposition."

Her brother chuckled. "You always were a tiger for her cubs. He has no idea what he's letting himself in for."

"But I do. I never much liked London Society, Matty. I could never find my footing. I know how to care for little girls. I like to think I'm good at it."

"You are." His voice was soft. "Daisy and Tuny are credits to you. They miss you."

Her heart tightened, pushing a lump into her throat. "I miss them too. I think of you all often. Perhaps they can come visit, when the Season is over."

"Daisy tells me you're hosting a house party."

So, her sister couldn't be bothered to explain to him why Ivy had left, but she was all too happy to claim an upcoming party. Ivy had already determined why the letter had gone missing. She'd told Daisy the note explained everything. Very likely Daisy thought that included her prank, which had locked Ivy and Kendall in Lord Carrolton's library. Her sister should have known better. Ivy wasn't about to share that particular story. Kendall could well think she'd conspired with Daisy to trap him.

"We are not hosting a house party," she told her brother. "Disabuse her of that thought at once."

He shrugged. "You know Daisy. Once she gets an idea in her head, it's hard to dislodge it. You aren't so different. I'm not sure I'd have counseled you to accept his lordship's proposal, just for a mess of porridge."

"It's rather nice porridge," Ivy said with a smile. "And Matty, I can help Daisy and Tuny. I can give them dowries."

He stepped back. "That's my duty."

"And you need to provide for a wife and someday

children," she reminded him. "Let me help Daisy and Tuny."

"Still thinking like their mother," he pointed out.

"And I likely will to my dying day," Ivy replied. "I want the best for them. I love you all."

"Do you love him?"

She shouldn't tell him the truth about their arrangement. Kendall had no expectations of her save that she mother Sophia. But just once, just with her beloved brother, she wanted to share her heart.

"Yes, Matthew," she said. "Perhaps not as extravagantly as some, but I do. I think I have since the day he first offered to dance with me. And do not ask whether he loves me. I know the answer. He loved his first wife. He believes, once having loved, he has nothing more to give."

"Mad," Matthew said. "Absolutely raving."

"Sad," Ivy argued. "So very filled with sorrow. Imagine how you'd feel if you lost Charlotte. Would you want to look at another woman?"

He rubbed the back of his neck. "I never thought to love a woman as fine as Charlotte. There will never be her equal."

The arrow struck her heart. But she had to hope—for Sophia, for Kendall, for herself. Ivy lay a hand on his as he lowered it. "Give him time. He may come to cherish me as I do him."

Matthew shook his head. "I know what the nobs will say: he's too good for you. They're wrong, Ivy. You're far too good for Lord Kendall, and he better realize it soon, or we really will have words."

The next few days passed pleasantly. Ivy and Kendall saw Matthew off in the morning, and Ivy caught Travis bearing off the nightshirt as if he intended to have it bronzed. Her anise biscuits met with much success. She was certain she heard a groan of pleasure from Kendall as he took the first bite. Perhaps her favorite part of each day, however, was after tea, when Sophia was napping, and Ivy would take walks with Kendall.

After their walk the day Matthew had arrived, Kendall seemed to expect Ivy to accompany him. She certainly wasn't going to protest. Away from his duties, he seemed more relaxed, willing to share their lives. They strolled through the formal gardens at the front of the house and the less formal plantings behind it. They walked to each of the rivers, discussed the merits of the stream, the dangers it could pose to those living nearby. They visited the farm at the very south of the estate, where Kendall discovered they did indeed have chickens. And always they talked, about the future, and about their pasts.

"You say little about your father," he commented the third day as they walked to the north, where a folly—square and squat—looked up at the house from a precise angle. "Sir Matthew mentioned he began acting as head of the house when he was still a lad."

Oh, how she hated discussing things that might encourage him to think less of her and her family. "As I told you, our father worked a great deal. You understand the responsibility of providing for a family."

"Indeed." He kept his gaze on their destination, the white stone building surrounded by willows. "I am blessed not to have to toil to do so. I cannot imagine having no time to spend with my child."

Ivy stopped on the graveled path, drew in a breath of the warm summer air. "He had time. He chose to use it to drink himself into a stupor. He'd been hurt, at the mill," she hurried to add as Kendall glanced her way, frown gathering. "There was nothing that could be done, and he needed to keep working. Drinking was his way of escape.

We all understood, even if we didn't like it."

He took her hand, his fingers strong and warm, as if sunlight had infused them. "He was fortunate to have your love."

"I think he knew that, deep down," Ivy said, relishing the feel of his hand on hers. "And he did try to give us a mother, for all he chose the wrong person."

"Ah, yes, this stepmother," he said. "None of you are fond of her."

Not fond. A very polite way of collecting all the troublesome emotions surrounding Mrs. Bateman. Perhaps it was the feel of his hand that made some of those emotions tumble out now. "She made us her servants. Matthew had left home by then. He sent money for our care. She found other uses for it."

And there came the bitterness she fought so hard against. She didn't want to be that person. She straightened, and her hand slipped out of his. "She was an unhappy woman who chose to make others unhappy. I do not intend to follow her example."

"You don't have it in you to follow such an example," he said. "I have never met anyone like you, Ivy."

She wanted to hug his praise close, but she couldn't quite believe it. "Not even Lady Kendall?" she asked.

He started walking again, voice as soft as his look. "Adelaide had a different focus."

The polite response did not satisfy. "Oh?" Ivy pressed. "In what way?"

"We'd known each other most of our lives; our parents were good friends," he explained. "So I understood when I married her that health was always fleeting. That didn't stop us from falling in love. We had so much in common."

Unlike the two of them, but Ivy merely nodded as they approached the willows, their draperies a contrast to the firm lines of the stone folly.

"You have only to look at Sophia to see her nature," he

continued, hands brushing the silvery green fronds. "Frail, yet inquisitive, happy. She was the love of my life, and my best friend."

What a blow. Her heart ached just imagining it. She wanted to reach out, gather him close, but she didn't think he would allow it. "I'm very sorry for your loss," she said instead.

"I will always miss her." His voice was so heavy she regretted even bringing up the subject. "I should have realized carrying a child would be too much for her, but we both wanted children. And I could never refuse her anything."

Ivy had to take his hand, cradling it in hers. "You mustn't blame yourself. You said she was frail. She must have understood the dangers."

He stopped, one foot up on the steps leading to the folly and gaze on their entwined fingers. "She did. And she would likely have gone through it even knowing what lay ahead, just to give Sophia life. She would have made a wonderful mother."

His voice had thickened, and tears sparkled on his sable lashes. All of her hurt.

"And you have the makings of a wonderful father," Ivy assured him, giving his hand a squeeze. "And when Sophia is old enough to understand, we will tell her all about her mother and the love that bore her."

He nodded and lifted her hand to his lips for a kiss.

The sweet pressure worked its way through her, and she bit her lip to stop herself from crying out how she felt about him right there and then. It seemed wrong to offer her love when his had been so cruelly taken. She must give him time.

He lowered her hand with a smile as watery as her own, and they climbed the steps to the folly, then turned and gazed at the house. But she held the memory of his kiss to her heart, hope growing that perhaps, someday, they too might share such a love.

CHAPTER FOURTEEN

Ivy's surprise at Kendall's kiss on her hand was nothing to the shock that reverberated through Villa Romanesque at the note which arrived the next day.

She was crossing the entry hall to take Sophia out for a little sunshine late that morning when she came across Mrs. Sheppard and Martha the elder near the hearth, hushed voices still carrying against all the stone surrounding them. Travis, on duty by the door, kept his gaze carefully away from them, as if hoping Ivy wouldn't notice.

"It's the duke's seal," Martha insisted, grey hair fluttering with her agitation. "I recognize it from when he sent messages to the previous Lord Kendall."

"But it's for Lady Kendall," Mrs. Sheppard protested. "This can only mean one thing."

"Is there a problem?" Ivy asked.

Both women spun and stared at her and Sophia, as if they'd been caught stealing some of her biscuits from the cooling rack.

The housekeeper recovered first. "No, indeed, your ladyship." She swept across the marble tiles to offer Ivy a wax-sealed note. She must have realized her fingers were trembling, for she raised her head and gripped the parchment tighter. Either that, or she simply didn't want to relinquish the note into Ivy's care.

"Hold Sophia a moment," Ivy said, and she traded the

baby for the note. Sophia frowned at the housekeeper, who held her out as if afraid she might break the baby, or the baby might break her.

Ivy snapped open the wax and unfolded the envelope. A card tumbled out to fall away from the note itself. Martha, who was hovering at the edge of their circle, bent to retrieve the card.

Ivy scanned down the note, most of which had been written in an elegant hand.

I would be remiss if I did not congratulate you on your nuptials. I hope I may call on you to welcome you to Surrey.

It was signed Eulalie Wey. But below the signature were words in another hand. *Good for you for marrying a marquess with a daughter and making a new family. I like you already. Jane.*

"News, your ladyship?" Mrs. Sheppard asked, angling her head as if to read the note herself.

Martha held out the card. "It's from the dowager duchess."

Mrs. Sheppard must have clasped Sophia hard, for the baby huffed in protest. "Get out the best china, Martha," the housekeeper ordered. "Travis, see that all the silver is polished. I will not tolerate a speck of dust on any surface."

Ivy lowered the note as the other staff members in the room turned white. "The dowager duchess did not provide a date."

"Nor will she," Mrs. Sheppard insisted, handing Sophia back to Ivy. "You must write back and tell her she is welcome to call at her earliest convenience." She seemed oblivious to the fact that she had just given her employer an order. "I'll speak to Mr. Sims about flowers from the garden. Her Grace favors lilies, if I'm not mistaken."

"Should we inform Lord Kendall?" Ivy asked, unsure whether to be amused or concerned by the amount of preparation required for a simple visit.

"Not yet," Mrs. Sheppard said, tapping her chin with one finger. "Not until we know the date. I'll need to alert his valet. No tweed."

Apparently, Her Grace had an aversion to the fabric. Ivy could only hope muslin and cambric suitable, for she didn't relish donning her wool this time of year.

"I can see this will involve strategy," she said. "I wouldn't dream of interfering. I have only one question. Who is Jane?"

Mrs. Sheppard blinked and dropped her hand. "Jane?"

"Yes." Ivy angled the note for the housekeeper to read, juggling Sophia to keep her from grabbing the parchment. "See? She writes in a different hand."

"Must be the new one," Martha muttered.

Mrs. Sheppard straightened. "The Duke of Wey remarried earlier this year."

"To his governess," Martha put in with a click of her tongue. "She was a cavalry officer's widow."

Mrs. Sheppard regarded her sternly. "That is quite enough. See to your duties, Martha."

With a drop of a curtsey, Martha hurried back to her work. The housekeeper turned to Ivy.

"Lady Kendall, I will see that appropriate stationery is provided for you to answer Her Grace. Becky can take charge of Lady Sophia while you write. I will have your response delivered straightaway. Perhaps Tuesday next might be appropriate for the visit."

Just for a moment, she considered refusing. Why should Tuesday, Ivy's baking day, be consigned to this visit? Why couldn't they just come tomorrow? It very much sounded as if the current duchess was like Ivy—a common woman who loved children and had been willing to marry their father to make a family again. And she recognized Ivy as her equal. How pleasant it would be to talk with someone who understood.

But Mrs. Sheppard was so determined to put on a good face. She fairly vibrated with her intentions now. If she needed five days to prepare, Ivy should give them to her.

"I'd be delighted," Ivy said.

"I don't suppose you have a card to send," Mrs. Sheppard said with a sigh, as if Ivy was severely lacking.

"Only in my maiden name," Ivy replied, glad Charlotte had insisted on the little pasteboard calling cards. "But I suppose I could write my new name over the top."

Mrs. Sheppard looked as aghast as if Ivy had suggested meeting the dowager duchess in her nightgown. "I sincerely hope that won't be necessary. I will write to the company that makes his lordship's and request a set for you. We'll have to answer Her Grace without one. She must not be kept waiting."

"Even if we had better things to do," Ivy told Sophia as she took the baby back upstairs to wait for *proper* paper. Did one need gilt-edged parchment to respond to a duchess? Ink infused with silver? Seals studded with jewels? She was a little surprised at the delicate pink parchment smelling faintly of roses that Travis brought up a short time later. It was not until she finished the note and given it to the footman to deliver that she realized something.

She wasn't nervous.

Mrs. Sheppard might scurry about, order her staff in every direction, but Ivy wasn't worried. Villa Romanesque was her home now. The duchess was coming to visit her. And she could hardly wait to meet Jane.

Kendall had ridden out that morning with his steward to see about some of the tenant cottages that needed repair following a wind earlier in the summer. The flat lands formed a channel through which not only water but air could flow. He agreed with his steward's assessment, assured his tenants the repairs would be made within the month, and rode back to Villa Romanesque to find the house in an uproar.

The drapes had been stripped from the entry hall windows. Martha the elder and another maid were down on their hands and knees scrubbing at the marble tiles. Travis, apron around his waist, was overseeing a team of underfootmen running feather dusters over all the walls.

"Have we had a fire?" Kendall asked him, concern rising.

"No, indeed, my lord," the head footman told him, pointing one of his underlings higher on the wall. "The Duchess of Wey is coming to call."

Kendall raised his brows, stepping aside as Martha passed him with her wash bucket. "Somehow I doubt Her Grace will notice the drapes in the entry hall."

"Her Grace will notice everything," Travis said. "Duchesses generally do."

Mrs. Sheppard seemed equally certain of the matter. She requested a moment of Kendall's time before he could go in search of Ivy. He led her to his study and took his place behind the desk.

"What seems to be the trouble, Mrs. Sheppard?" he asked.

"As you may have heard, my lord," she said, standing straight in front of him, gaze on the window over his left shoulder, "the Duchess of Wey intends to call. We have suggested next Tuesday."

Kendall leaned back. "I'm pleased to hear the duchess wishes to make Ivy's acquaintance."

"It is an honor." So much so that it propelled her a step forward. "A great honor. We must be ready."

"I see you are preparing," Kendall told her. "What do you need from me?"

"An increase in the household budget for the visit," she said, face tightening in her anxiety. "Her Grace favors Camho tea. I'll need to order it from London and have it delivered. I'd like to send all the drapes on the first floor to be laundered as well. We haven't the capacity. And we'll need to augment the staff."

It seemed a bit much for a short visit. The duchess had

no need to stay the night. His Grace's estate was only a couple hours ride to the northwest.

But he had never questioned Mrs. Sheppard's insights before. He waved a hand. "Whatever you need."

"And we must have something better than cinnamon buns," she burst out.

Kendall leaned back. "I am quite fond of those buns. But by all means, tell your new baker to concoct something more elaborate."

She shifted from foot to foot, gaze dropping to the pattern of the carpet. "I'm not sure she understands the gravity of this visit."

"She has been hired by a Great House," Kendall reminded her. "She had better learn."

"Perhaps a London baker, just this once?" Mrs. Sheppard begged, raising her gaze imploringly.

London was too far to go for any treat. Bakery items could well be stale or squashed before reaching Villa Romanesque. Mrs. Sheppard must know that. Why go to such trouble not to use this new baker of theirs?

Unless...

Sir Matthew had credited Ivy with the Naples biscuits when he had visited. She certainly seemed pleased anytime anyone mentioned the baked goods. Kendall had thought she was simply proud of an employee she had advised, but there was another possibility.

Could Ivy be the new baker?

He leaned back in his chair. "Perhaps I should speak to our baker, impress upon her the importance of this visit."

Mrs. Sheppard blanched. "No, no. That is my duty."

Kendall stood, surety growing with every word. "Nonsense. I'm the master of this house. If she will not listen to you, she had better listen to me." He started around the desk, and his housekeeper scurried to block his way forward.

"Please, my lord. She is a dear. I wouldn't want to hurt

her for the world."

Her eyes were bright, her hands clasped before her grey gown. But was it Ivy's reputation or her own she sought to protect?

"Is Lady Kendall baking?" he demanded. "Do not lie to me. You know she'll admit it if I ask her."

She slumped. "Yes, my lord. I tried to dissuade her."

Very likely she had. What a scandal that the lady of Villa Romanesque dirtied her hands in the kitchen. This pastime would only add fuel to the rumors that he had married her to make her a servant in his house, caring for his daughter, baking in his kitchen. Some would find even more reason not to associate with her.

"And you deem this shameful," he accused his housekeeper.

Once more Mrs. Sheppard shuffled her feet. "I did, my lord, but how can I refuse her? She loves it so. Her entire countenance glows as she mixes things together. And the staff love that she bakes enough for them too."

She would. Ivy was nothing if not generous, with her time, with her talents.

With her love.

"You won't stop her, will you?" Mrs. Sheppard asked as if she'd seen something in his face. "We don't have to let anyone else know. It truly isn't as shameful as I'd feared. Some ladies tend their own gardens."

She waited, clearly expecting him to protest, expecting contempt for Ivy's shocking lack of protocol. Adelaide would never have set foot in the kitchen, never have dreamed of trying to bake something that would please Kendall, much less the staff. He knew what his father would advise.

And he knew what he must do.

"I want Ivy to be happy at Villa Romanesque," Kendall told his housekeeper. "I wouldn't dream of stopping her. On the contrary, I'd like to encourage her in something she clearly enjoys and excels at. Tell me what else she might need in the kitchen, and I'll see the very best examples delivered within the week. And as for the upcoming visit, I see no need to send to London. The dowager duchess should be so fortunate as to eat some of Ivy's creations."

CHAPTER FIFTEEN

The dowager duchess and her daughter-in-law arrived on Tuesday in two elegantly appointed carriages. One held the dowager and her maid. The other held the current duchess and the duke's three daughters. The only sign that Mrs. Sheppard was displeased to have the children along was the pinch of her nostrils. Ivy was only sad she'd arranged Sophia's schedule so that the little girl would nap through the better part of the visit. Mrs. Sheppard had already expressed her displeasure that Kendall had been called to the village on some issue requiring his attendance as magistrate.

"As if civil unrest were more important than a visit from Her Grace," Ivy had heard her mutter to Travis.

And so Ivy stood in the marble entry hall, dressed in her best silk day gown, a soft rose, to greet their exalted guests.

"Welcome to Villa Romanesque, Your Graces," she said as they all entered the hall to be surrounded by footmen and maids accepting shawls and bonnets. Even three ladies, three children ranging from six to eleven, and six servants didn't manage to make the space feel crowded. It did, however, make it feel more like home.

Perhaps it was the smile on the face of the younger duchess. She was built sturdily, with thick brown hair that had managed to escape the bun at the back of her head and wide brown eyes. Her cambric gown was embroidered all over with bright yellow daisies, and the shawl she decided to keep with her was a sunny yellow as well.

She came up to Ivy and stuck out her hand. "Welcome to the neighborhood. I'm Jane, Duchess of Wey. I hope you'll leave off the Your Grace business and just call me Jane."

"Of course, Jane," Ivy said with a smile, shaking a hand that seemed too firm to have belonged to a duchess for long. "You must call me Ivy."

She beamed, then leaned closer to whisper. "You'll have to call Her Grace Her Grace. She insists upon it." Straightening, she turned to her mother-in-law. "Your Grace, may I present Ivy, Marchioness of Kendall?"

The dowager duchess, a thoroughly elegant woman in a dove grey gown fitted to her slender form, inclined her head. "A pleasure, Lady Kendall. I've known your husband since he was a boy. I'm glad to see he has continued with his life after that terrible business with the previous Lady Kendall."

"And she will mention a tragedy or two," Jane warned in a whisper. Loudly, she said, "These are my daughters. Lady Larissa—"

The tallest, most regal little girl, inclined her head, setting her light brown hair to gleaming. Her gown of lavender lustring strewn with lace and satin ribbon might have graced a princess.

"Lady Calantha, she prefers Callie—"

The slender towhead in a more sensible blue cambric gown bobbed a curtsey.

"And Lady Abelona. She likes Belle."

"And unicorns," the youngest insisted, golden curls bouncing along with the ruffles on her white muslin gown.

The dowager duchess smiled at her granddaughter, then turned to Ivy. "I hope you don't mind the children, Lady Kendall. Jane and I thought the experience of visiting you would prove edifying."

Edifying. As if meeting her was a great honor.

"I'm delighted you brought them along," Ivy assured her. "I have a sister about your age, Lady Larissa. Perhaps you will meet when she comes to visit this summer."

Lady Larissa put her fine-boned nose in the air. "I'm not at all certain that would be suitable."

Ivy frowned, then noticed the girl's sister was staring at Ivy.

"Grandmother says you're the daughter of a merchant," Callie said. "Mother's father was a vicar."

The dowager's sculpted cheeks were turning pink even as Mrs. Sheppard attempted to blend into the wall. "What have we told you, Calantha," her grandmother asked, "about reporting everything you hear?"

Callie hung her head. "Not every conversation was meant to be shared."

"And your grandmother is wrong," Ivy said. "My father wasn't a merchant. He was a millworker. And my brother is a famous pugilist once called the Beast of Birmingham."

She wasn't sure why she admitted it. Very likely the wiser choice would have been to shrink back like Mrs. Sheppard and say as little as possible. Indeed, both the dowager duchess and Lady Larissa were gaping at her.

Jane reached out and clapped her on the shoulder. "I knew I'd like you! We must talk boxing. Callie is interested in taking up the sport."

"Purely for the purposes of healthful exercise," the dowager assured everyone as Mrs. Sheppard hurried toward the emerald salon to open the doors for them.

Thankful for Jane, Ivy led them down to the room where everything had been prepared. Sunlight trickled past emerald draperies newly cleaned, pressed, and rehung. The dowager duchess' favorite tea was already steeping in the pot, a scent like violets wafting up from the steaming silver spout. Ivy's baked goods sat on fine china plates edged in silver. Damask napkins embroidered at the corners with an emerald K waited to be placed on the laps of their guests.

Mrs. Sheppard waited by one of the urns, hands alternately rising and dropping, as if she wished to usher each person into a special seat. Ivy ignored her and allowed her guests to sit where it pleased them—Jane with Callie and Belle on either side on the curved-back sofa and Larissa on an upholstered chair near her grandmother. Ivy took up her place at the tea cart. The housekeeper might serve tea to Ivy and Kendall, but Ivy was the hostess now. And she actually had good tea to deal out, tea she had told Mrs. Sheppard to consider in the future, if the household budget would stretch so far.

Conversation flowed with the brew. Indeed, she was surprised how many things they found to discuss—the flooding that plagued the area in the spring, the type of tea best served in the summer, the cost of importing items from London, the instruction of children. Jane dominated the conversation, her brown eyes alight, her smile engaging. She was very good about including everyone from the dowager duchess to little Belle. She even threw a question or two to Mrs. Sheppard and Travis, who were on duty to assist. Her effort seemed to both please and confuse the housekeeper.

"May I have another cake?" Callie asked with a longing look at the tea cart. Mrs. Sheppard had made no complaint when Ivy had attempted a more elaborate set of dishes for the tea, including tiny vanilla cakes with pineapple icing, almond cheesecakes, and lemon biscuits along with her favorite cinnamon buns. She decided not to point out to the housekeeper that her cinnamon buns were the most sampled.

"That's enough for now, Callie," Jane told her with a smile. "Though perhaps Lady Kendall will allow us to take some home."

All three girls brightened at that.

"Quite delectable," the dowager agreed, pausing to

nibble on a lemon biscuit. "Our cook has never managed anything this light. Did you send away to London?"

"No," Ivy said, feeling Mrs. Sheppard tense. "We have our own baker."

"Perhaps we can borrow him from time to time," the dowager mused.

Mrs. Sheppard collapsed against the wall, then hastily straightened again.

"I would be delighted to send you as many treats as you'd like," Ivy said. "If there's something special you prefer, just let us know."

The dowager turned to Jane. "Perhaps we could put in an order for the wedding."

"We are hosting a wedding ceremony and breakfast for Miss Meredith Thorn and her betrothed, Julian Mayes," Jane explained. "I saw your name on the guest list, Ivy."

"I haven't received an invitation yet," Ivy said. "But I know Miss Thorn well. She chaperoned me and my sister part of the Season. She introduced my brother, Matthew, to his bride, Charlotte Worthington. I'd be delighted to contribute to the event in any way I can."

They talked a while longer before the dowager rose, signaling that it was time to take their leave. Jane made Ivy promise to return the visit as soon as possible. Ivy walked them to the carriages, Mrs. Sheppard and Travis right behind, and waved as her new friends trundled down the drive. She'd survived her first visit, and in rather fine style, she thought.

She turned to find Mrs. Sheppard frowning at her. Ivy's stomach sank. "What did I do wrong?"

Mrs. Sheppard's face cleared. "Nothing, your ladyship. The dowager duchess and Her Grace, the Duchess of Wey, seemed pleased with their visit."

Ivy drew in a breath. "Oh, good. And I thought we fended off the issue of the baker well."

"Exceedingly well," the housekeeper agreed, falling into

step beside her as Travis returned to his place by the door. "May I speak to you a moment before you go to Lady Sophia?"

Perhaps she wasn't out of the woods just yet.

"Of course," Ivy said.

Mrs. Sheppard led her to Ivy's suite and made sure to shut the door to the corridor and the one to Sophia's room, where Becky was mending a frock in the rocker while the baby napped.

The housekeeper turned to face Ivy and drew in an audible breath. "I must apologize, your ladyship."

Ivy's brows lifted. "Apologize? Why?"

Mrs. Sheppard was worrying her hands before her neat grey gown. "I have, perhaps, been overly focused on the honor of hosting the first family of the region."

"I understand," Ivy assured her. "You wanted to make a good impression."

"I wanted to make the best impression," Mrs. Sheppard corrected her, "because I was certain you would make a poor one."

Though she had suspected as much, hearing it said aloud hurt. "I see."

"That's why I must apologize," the housekeeper insisted. "You are nothing but a credit to Villa Romanesque. I had no right to assume otherwise or to take your place in the preparations. If you would like me to tender my resignation, I will do so."

She dropped her hands, back straight, head high: a condemned criminal walking toward the gallows. Ivy would never have pulled the lever to hang her.

"You are a valued part of this household, Mrs. Sheppard," she said. "I would no more discharge you than paint the emerald salon pink."

The housekeeper managed a smile. "Thank you, your ladyship."

"Lord Kendall and Sophia deserve a house that is well

run, clean, and pleasing to the eye," Ivy continued. "We all rely on you to provide that. I will help however I can, but if I am ever in a position to hinder that, you must let me know."

Mrs. Sheppard curtsied. "As you wish, your ladyship." She straightened and took a step closer to Ivy. "Now, how are we to manage baking for this wedding?"

Meredith was preparing to go out for the afternoon. Lydia had invited her over to see the latest progress on the balloon, and they planned to take tea with Yvette afterward. She was pulling up her lavender gloves as she descended the stair, Fortune padding along hopefully beside her, when she spotted Mr. Cowls standing in the entryway. He had been her family butler when she was a child. He had come out of retirement to serve her now. She fully intended him to attend her wedding, along with Cook and Enid, her maid, who had joined her since she'd received the inheritance.

Now the look on his lined face under his pomaded white hair could only be called severe.

"What's happened?" Meredith asked as she reached his side.

Fortune wound around his ankles as if offering support.

His long nose gave a twitch, as if he'd smelled something distasteful. "There is a stranger speaking to Cook. Would you like me to throw him out, or would you prefer to ask him his business first?"

Meredith frowned. "A stranger? A beggar you mean?"

"Likely not, madam. Beggars generally do not ask such leading questions."

Fortune returned to Meredith's side, tail up, as if now aligning herself for battle.

NEVER MARRY A MARQUESS 149

"I see no reason for anyone to be asking my staff leading questions," Meredith informed her butler. "Why didn't you call a constable, send for a Bow Street Runner to investigate?"

Mr. Cowls's gaze was well above her head. "I have reason to believe he is a Bow Street Runner, madam."

Ice raced up her spine. Meredith picked up her lavender skirts and swept down the corridor for the kitchen. Fortune stalked at her side.

As her butler had said, a fellow with a pocked face and thick brown hair half hidden by a tweed cap leaned against the doorjamb to the rear garden.

"Sounds like a fine lady to be working for," he was telling Cook, who was finishing her supper preparations as she chatted with the investigator assigned to the Bow Street magistrate's office, their pot boy sitting with hands wet from the scrubbing to listen. "But I heard her fortune came to her in scandal."

"No," Cook said, knife slicing through a carrot. "Fortune attached herself to the mistress some time ago."

He blinked in obvious confusion, then straightened as Meredith moved into the room.

"What do you think you're doing, disturbing my staff?" she demanded.

He touched his cap. "Beggin' your pardon, ma'am. Just looking for a friendly ear."

"An earful of gossip, you mean," Meredith countered. She bent and scooped up Fortune before the cat could escape past his legs into the walled garden beyond. "Why are you here? Who asked you to look into my affairs?"

He held up his hands. "Now, then, no complaint's been made to the magistrate. I'm simply asking for a friend."

Meredith glared at him. "What friend?"

He lowered his hands. "Wouldn't be much of one if I named names. Suffice it to say, a man deserves to know who he's marrying, Miss Rose."

The sound of that name never failed to stab her. Did he know it? And why insinuate Julian had set him to this questioning? Julian knew all about her past. He had no reason to wonder about her. Did he?

She glanced up at the fellow. Those green eyes were shrewd, watching her, assessing.

"And you've made a mistake," she told him. "There is no Miss Rose in this house. If I hear of you bothering my staff or acquaintances again, I will speak to the magistrate myself. Now, begone."

Fortune put back her ears and hissed at him.

The Runner backed away. Meredith watched until he turned and let himself out of the gate.

"Wait a moment, then follow him," Mr. Cowls told their pot boy. "I want to know his client."

"Yes, sir. I'll try." The boy shook the suds off his hands and crept out the door.

"Forgive me, madam," Cook said, gaze on the tiles of the floor. "I didn't mean to gossip. He came to the door looking for scraps, he said. I just thought it would be kind to pass the time."

He'd been looking for scraps, all right, anything he could find that put Meredith in a dismal light. Why? She'd kept to herself before agreeing to Julian's courtship. Her clients were all happy with her support—look how quickly they'd accepted her wedding invitation.

No, this Runner had to have come on the behest of the same person who'd sent someone to question Sir Harry and his staff about Patience. Surely not Julian. Julian loved her, was going to link his life to hers. So who had decided to probe into her background now? And what were they hoping to find?

Worse, were her clients in danger?

She whirled to face her butler. "Send word to Lady Worthington that I will be delayed. I must write to Jane, Patience, Charlotte, and Ivy. Have someone ready to take the notes as soon as I finish. I'll alert Lydia and Yvette when I see them. And send word to Mr. Mayes to call this evening. Someone is trying to hurt us, and I won't allow it."

CHAPTER SIXTEEN

Ivy ran her hand over the gleaming copper pan. "And you say Lord Kendall ordered these?"

"To encourage our new baker," Mrs. Sheppard told her as they stood in the busy kitchen. "Along with four sheets, a set of porcelain mixing bowls, and a rolling pin. And I wonder—what would you think of a Rumford range?"

"I'd be ever so grateful, your ladyship," Mrs. Grunion said with a wistful sigh that loosened the apron on her chest.

Ivy had heard of the invention. Instead of juggling pots in the hearth, a lady could use a Rumford range to cook each pot in a long row, with the heat regulated under each pot. To think of such a wonder, in her kitchen!

Ivy lowered her hand. "It would be marvelous, Mrs. Grunion, but I cannot justify the expense. Even these may be too much. Perhaps we should send them back."

Mrs. Grunion's round face fell, and the housekeeper caught Ivy's hand as if fearing she meant to snatch up the new items right then. She must have remembered her place, for she quickly dropped her hand. But she didn't give up on her quest.

"Please, your ladyship, don't refuse the gifts. He was so delighted to help."

Ivy's heart softened. "Very well. Thank you for your input, Mrs. Grunion. Mrs. Sheppard, may I have a word?"

The housekeeper followed her out into the corridor,

shutting the door on the cook's curious gaze.

"You won't speak to him," Mrs. Sheppard said as they started down the corridor. "It would spoil his joy in surprising the baker."

"Not today," Ivy promised her. "But I wanted to talk to you about the household budget. If we mean to invest in new pans and such, we must economize elsewhere. Ask Mrs. Grunion to make soup the main course at least once a week, and no more sending to London for meat and vegetables. We can buy from local farmers."

Mrs. Sheppard frowned. "Are we having financial difficulties, my lady?"

"Not yet," Ivy said. "And I'd like to keep it that way. Besides, there's all the ingredients we'll need to bake for Miss Thorn's wedding."

"I'll see to it," the housekeeper assured her. "I can move things around in the household budget."

"Good," Ivy said as they reached the entry hall. "Now, another question. The Duchess of Wey mentioned an invitation that should have arrived for me from Miss Thorn. Do you know what might have become of it?"

Mrs. Sheppard glanced to Travis beside the door. "I'll look into the matter, your ladyship, and ensure any correspondence is delivered to you immediately."

Ivy thanked her and headed upstairs for Kendall's daily visit with Sophia.

She had suggested that he spend more time with his daughter each day and was doing what she could to see those visits successful, for him and for Sophia. She'd looked through the old nursery and located several clapboard books, the hand-tinted colors mellowed with time, as well as a few toys that might suit a baby. Now she seated Kendall in the oak rocker and brought him his daughter and a book.

He accepted Sophia carefully but eyed the book with a frown. "What am I to do with that?"

"Read to her," Ivy said as Sophia reached for the book.

"I need both hands to keep her safe," he protested.

Perhaps not safe, but certainly secure. Already Sophia was wiggling against her father's grip, which was obviously tightening.

"Watch me," Ivy said. She took the baby back from him and went to sit on the other chair in the room. "Balance her on your knee like so, and put one arm around her back, your hand on her hip. She is well anchored, but still capable of moving so she won't resist confinement."

He stood and wandered closer. "Ingenious," he murmured as if she'd been the first mother to think of the tactic.

"Hold the book in your other hand. These pages are thick enough you could let her turn them herself." She lifted the book and spread the pages with her fingers. Sophia's eyes widened as she gazed at the picture.

"Ride a cock-horse to Banbury cross," Ivy read, "to see a fine lady upon a white horse. Rings on her fingers and bells on her toes, she shall have music wherever she goes."

Sophia leaned forward and reached for the book.

Kendall flung himself at her. "She'll fall!"

Sophia took one look at his concerned face and broke into wails. He collapsed back, concern turning to dismay.

"Go sit on the rocker," Ivy told him kindly.

She could feel his reluctance. Very likely few people ever ordered him about, even in kind tones. She certainly wouldn't have dreamed of it a month ago, but someone had to intervene between him and Sophia. Still, he went and sat, so stiffly he might have been made of oak too. Ivy brought him the sobbing baby.

"Hold her close, pat her back," she instructed him. "Talk to her."

He settled Sophia against him, but he could not seem to bring himself to lift his hand off her and pat her. "Lovely weather we're having," he said.

Sophia gulped down a cry, then stuck a thumb in her

mouth.

He thrust her back. "Do you see that? She's starving. When was she last fed?"

Sophia started crying again.

"She was fed an hour ago," Ivy told him. "She isn't starving. Babies suck their thumbs to comfort themselves."

Kendall gazed at his sobbing daughter. "Which means I failed to bring her comfort."

"Try again," Ivy urged. "Show her how much you love her."

It was as if she'd lit a fire in a cold, dark room. His look softened, his countenance warmed. He cuddled his little girl, set the rocker in motion. Sophia lay her head against his chest and sighed contentedly, cries dwindling to a hiccough.

He gazed down at her dark head in obvious awe. "There's Papa's little darling. Everything will be all right. I promise."

Sophia's eyes drifted shut.

Ivy's heart soared. This, this moment was why she was in this house, why she'd agreed to marry him. She wanted to hold them both close, share the love that glowed around them.

Would there ever come a time when she was held in those arms, when Kendall whispered words of love meant only between a husband and wife?

She was showing him how to be a father. Could she show him what it meant to be a husband again?

Daring thought, but it refused to leave her over the next few days. They were coming to know each other well. Did he notice nothing to encourage him closer? Was there something she was willing to change that might make him see her differently? Was it right to encourage him closer when she'd agreed to a marriage of convenience?

She hadn't realized her internal debate was showing externally until Mrs. Sheppard asked for a moment of her time while Sophia was being changed and Kendall closeted with his steward.

"Is there a problem with the household staff?" the housekeeper asked, face bunching in concern, as she addressed Ivy in her suite.

"No, certainly not," Ivy assured her. "You've all been wonderful."

"Then perhaps the decor fails to please her ladyship?" Mrs. Sheppard persisted, wandering over to tug the drapes wider. "More flowers in the rooms? Different varieties? New paintings?"

"The house is beautiful," Ivy told her. "Have I done something to indicate otherwise?"

"Not in so many words," the housekeeper allowed, returning to her spot on the deep green carpet. "But, if I may say so, your ladyship seems unaccountably pensive of late. The staff is concerned."

The thought that the busy staff would notice, and care, touched her heart. "Thank you all for your kindness," Ivy said with a smile, "but I'm fine. Perhaps just considering my role at Villa Romanesque."

Mrs. Sheppard drew herself up. "You are the lady of the manor. I defy anyone to say otherwise."

What a champion she'd gained in the housekeeper. Perhaps enough of a champion to appeal to for help now?

Ivy eyed her. "You knew the previous lady of the manor, Lord Kendall's first wife."

Mrs. Sheppard shifted, grey skirts swinging, as if the mention of the deceased troubled her. "I did. And Lord Kendall's mother before her."

Ivy spread her hands. "What can I do to be more like them?"

"Why would you want to be more like them?" Mrs. Sheppard demanded. As Ivy reared back, the housekeeper pressed two fingers to her lips.

"Forgive me, Lady Kendall," she said, lowering her hand. "That was not my place. I meant no disrespect to those ladies, God rest their souls. It's simply that you are a different sort of person."

Her shoulders felt so heavy she could only let her hands fall. "Then there is no hope for me."

Mrs. Sheppard took a step forward, eyes narrowing. "You mistake me. Lord Kendall's mother was a tyrant who spent every moment ruling her son and her husband with an iron hand. The previous Lord Kendall praised her devotion, but I think the poor man grew five inches after she was gone. The last Lady Kendall was as frail as a butterfly. She had to focus on her own needs merely to survive, so a certain self-interest was to be expected. You are stronger, kinder, and more compassionate than both of them combined. Do not try to be their equal. You are already far superior."

Ivy's lips were trembling, and she had to stop herself from hugging the housekeeper. "Oh, Mrs. Sheppard, thank you. You cannot know what your words mean to me. If only Lord Kendall saw me the same way."

"Ah." The housekeeper stepped back. "That is easily remedied. I will have a word with Percy about your hair."

Ivy's hand flew to the bun at the top of her head. "My hair?"

"Just gilding the lily," Mrs. Sheppard assured her. "A few changes in wardrobe and accessories will make all the difference. Percy will know what to do."

Ivy swallowed, lowering her hand. "Might there be someone other than Percy who could provide advice? I'm not sure she likes me much."

The housekeeper's lips tightened. "She is being well paid to serve you. If she doesn't enjoy the duty, she can find other work. Leave this to me, your ladyship. We will show Lord Kendall the gem you are, and I have no doubt he will come to appreciate you as much as we all do."

Kendall breathed deep of the warm summer breeze as he and his steward returned from reviewing the progress on reroofing the tenant cottages. His tenants were pleased; his steward was pleased. He had every reason to be pleased as well, if for an entirely different reason.

He was coming to know his daughter.

What an amazing creature! So curious, so clever. Just the other day she'd begun spouting syllables. They hadn't added up to words, yet, but Ivy said it was only moments before Sophia said *Papa*. That would likely be one of the finest days of his life.

Doctor Penrose had been equally delighted.

"Stronger than she's ever been," he'd said at his last visit. "Lungs and heart sound good, and her weight and height are approaching what I would expect for her age. I believe it safe for me to call once a month. Your staff is to be congratulated."

It wasn't the staff. It was Ivy. Her care of Sophia was nothing short of brilliant. He could not imagine life without her.

Except when he looked at Sophia and saw Adelaide looking back at him. Then he felt small, lacking. He had promised to love Adelaide with all his heart. Was it right that now, more often, his thoughts veered to Ivy?

"Looks like we have a visitor," his steward said with a nod toward the drive. Kendall recognized the coach and urged his gelding faster.

Sir Alexander was just alighting, satchel under one arm.

"My lord, well met," he said, as Kendall reined in and dismounted. "I've brought those papers we discussed. If I could have a moment of your and the lady's time, we can sign them, and I'll be off."

The steward excused himself, a groom took charge of Kendall's horse, and Kendall accompanied the solicitor into the house, directing him to the study while he sent

Travis to locate Ivy. Then he joined his man of affairs.

Mrs. Sheppard brought lemonade and biscuits and curtsied before leaving them. Sir Alexander poured himself a glass.

"I hope Lady Sophia remains well," the solicitor said, holding the sweating crystal in his hands.

"She is in the best possible health," Kendall told him, pouring himself a glass as well as he sat next to his man. "Better than ever before. She is about ready to crawl. Ivy says there will be no stopping her then."

Alex rolled the glass back and forth between his palms. "Lady Kendall spends a great deal of time with the girl, I take it?"

Why did he make that sound distressing? Did he feel Kendall had taken advantage of Ivy's good nature? There were moments Kendall wondered.

"Ivy is devoted to her," he told the solicitor. "Sophia would not have come so far, so quickly, without her. I am certain of that."

"Well," Alex allowed, leaning back, "they say babies are indiscriminate creatures. So long as you find a proper governess before Lady Sophia is too old, I'm sure she will still grow up to be her mother's daughter."

Immediately his guilt began whispering. *You see? Even Alex knows you must do more to honor Adelaide's memory.*

Ivy entered just then, and Kendall set down his glass to rise and meet her. Alex stood more slowly, setting aside his glass and going around to take his place behind the desk, for all the world as if they had come to see him at his office.

Kendall shoved aside the mild irritation at the gesture. Alex was nothing if not efficient. It would be easier if Kendall and Ivy were standing together.

"Sir Alex would like us to sign the dower arrangements," Kendall explained as he reached Ivy's side. "It shouldn't take long."

She smiled, like sunlight brightening his study, and he

could not help but admire the way the rose-colored gown matched the shade of her lips. She had always been lovely, but lately something had changed. Her hair seemed softer, little tendrils brushing her cheeks, the color more golden. And he hadn't realized just how impressive her figure was until she'd tied a sash under her bosom.

Admiration. Just admiration.

He stuck out his arm for her to take and kept her a stately distance away from him as he escorted her to the desk and released her.

Alex had spread the pages out for them. "Everything as we agreed, my lord. A generous dower arrangement—house of her own, funds to support herself. The usual sort of thing."

Kendall glanced over the closely written pages, noting all the provisions he'd specified, except one. "Where are the dowries for Ivy's sisters?"

Ivy put a hand on his arm. "Sir Alexander explained to me the impropriety of the offer."

Kendall glanced up at the solicitor, who was smiling pleasantly. "What impropriety?"

Alex waved a hand. "Tongues will wag if a lady is given more than what might be expected. I merely thought to protect Lady Kendall from such a calamity. If you would both sign, my lord, I will take myself off and leave you to your pleasures."

Ivy picked up the quill.

Kendall reached out to stop her before she could dip it in ink. "I agreed to support Lady Kendall's sisters," he insisted. "The papers must be redrawn."

She bit her lip, glancing between him and the solicitor. "But the expense. I would not deprive you and Sophia for the world."

So that was her concern. Kendall touched her cheek, the skin soft and warm. "My dear, there is no deprivation. I have money to spare."

NEVER MARRY A MARQUESS

"Money that the estate needs, my lord," Alex put in. "You have, perhaps, been preoccupied with Lady Sophia, but you have requirements that must be met."

Kendall dropped his hand and turned to his solicitor with a frown. "What are you talking about? We have no mortgage, no debt."

"For now," Alex said unhelpfully. "But improvements will be needed. You will want to continue your family's legacy in Roman antiquities. Then there are these excessive amounts going to the household account—the money will have to come from somewhere."

Ivy flinched, hands pressing against her diaphragm as if trying to hold back her breathless reply.

"Do you know something about our finances you haven't shared with me, sir?" Kendall demanded. "Because the last time I consulted the ledger, there was no reason for concern."

Alex waved a hand. "I would not trouble you with trivialities, my lord. Suffice it to say, I have endeavored to ensure Villa Romanesque can continue for another generation without hardship. But it is always wise to consider what might be recouped from an investment. You must admit, it is doubtful the Bateman sisters could be expected to marry well, even with dowries."

Ivy raised her head, cheeks pinking. "How dare you, sir."

"Leave," Kendall said. "Now."

Ivy stared at him, as if he had spoken to her. Alex must have thought so as well, for he was clearly struggling not to smile. Kendall met his gaze, fury squaring his shoulders. He might prefer to speak softly, to wield his power gently, but he had warned Alex and still the solicitor persisted in treating Ivy as if she were beneath him.

No one treated Ivy that way in his presence.

"Leave, I say, sirrah," he told the solicitor. "Get out of my house. My father hired your firm, so out of respect for him I will allow you to transfer management of my affairs to another of your staff, but I have no wish to speak to you again."

Alex gaped, but he recovered quickly. "My lord, I have always looked to the best interests of your family."

"By your words and attitude today, you make that statement a lie," Kendall told him. "Lady Kendall is my wife. Her family is my family. By belittling them, you belittle me. I will not stand for it."

Alex licked his lips. "I suppose an apology may be due."

"The fact that you only *suppose* proves how little that apology would mean. No, Sir Alexander, I am done with you."

Color flamed up him, but he grabbed his satchel and stalked from the room.

"Oh, Kendall!" Ivy cried, and she threw herself into his arms.

It was the easiest, most natural thing in the world to meet her lips with his own.

CHAPTER SEVENTEEN

He was kissing her. Ivy's surprise quickly blossomed into something more. His lips were warm, firm; the brush of his mustache like the caress of silk against her skin. She kissed him back, clung to him as joy and delight collided. She was one of the fireworks over Vauxhall, bursting in the night sky over the river, only the light, sound, and wonder were inside her.

He pulled back and stared at her, the same awed look she was becoming familiar with on his flushed face. "I beg your pardon."

Ivy seized his hand before he could withdraw further. "Don't. It was marvelous, wonderful. It gave me hope we might be more to each other one day."

His color washed away. "That was wrong of me, Ivy. Please forgive me." He pulled out of her grip. "I should change before we go see Sophia. Excuse me." He hurried from the room.

She could not be discouraged, not with her lips still tingling from his kiss. He had discharged a man long in his service because of a slight to her family. He had kissed her. She had a chance to win his heart.

She danced across to the door of the study, feet skimming the carpet. She had a chance. It might take time, it might take effort, but one day, she might truly be Kendall's wife.

It was very hard not to gaze at him besottedly as they

played with Sophia. Why had she never noticed the curved length of his lashes, sweeping his cheeks as he bent over the baby on the carpet? Or the way his smile lifted not only his lips but the edge of his mustache? Perhaps she had been staring overly long, for he glanced up at her expectantly.

"And what did you have planned this afternoon, Ivy?" he asked.

Another kiss?

Ivy settled her skirts around her to join him beside Sophia, face feeling warm. Among the toys she had brought down from the old nursery was a set of wooden blocks painted in bright colors. She spread them out in front of the baby now. Sophia promptly grabbed one and tried to put it in her mouth. Kendall snatched it away from her.

Sophia teared up.

"Build something," Ivy told Kendall, rubbing the little girl's shoulder.

He frowned at the jumble of color. "Build what?"

"Anything," Ivy said, "so long as it falls with a rattle."

His brow cleared as if he took her meaning, and he set to work with a will. How quick his hands, how sure. Hands that had touched her face and her heart, hands that held her effortlessly. She forced her attention back to Sophia, who was watching his progress avidly.

"There." He settled back on his haunches before an elegant tower.

Ivy moved the baby closer to it. "What do you think, Sophia?"

The little girl eyed the tower, then reached out a hand. Down it came with a clatter. She glanced between Ivy and Kendall.

Kendall clapped his hands. "Well done, my strong girl."

Sophia smiled and laughed.

"How do you think of such things?" Kendall asked after Sophia had demolished a dozen of his buildings, crowing with each crash. "I would never have thought to present blocks to a girl."

"Girls need to know they can control their world the same as boys," Ivy said. "Society may dictate our spheres, but it cannot rob us of our abilities."

"Or our pleasure in a job well done," he said. "You help me see the beauty of fatherhood, Ivy. Thank you."

His tender smile warmed her to her toes. As if he thought he'd overstepped once more, he busied himself with yet another tower.

Meredith paced the floor in her withdrawing room. Fortune darted out from hiding now and again to try to catch her lavender skirts as she passed. A shame she could not feel so lighthearted. Her former clients and friends had been as concerned as she was about the intrusion of this Bow Street Runner in their affairs.

"Gregory was not pleased to speak to him," Yvette had said when Meredith and Lydia had joined her for tea. The red-headed Frenchwoman's blue eyes twinkled. "Me? I had him followed, but he merely returned to the magistrate's office."

"Mr. Cowls had him followed as well," Meredith had explained, "with the same result."

Lydia glanced between them, pale blond ringlets bright around her creamy face. "Worth refused to see him. Too busy with his work. But I had a lovely chat on the way to the door. He's working for Sir Alexander Prentice, the solicitor."

Meredith had not been surprised the young viscountess had succeeded where she and Yvette had failed. With her big green eyes and eager conversation, Lydia was frequently underestimated by those who didn't know her well.

Meredith had expected some protest from Julian's former

mentor at their upcoming wedding but not an attack that would threaten her clients as well. It was a testament to the love her ladies and their gentlemen shared that none of the husbands had allowed the barbed questions to lodge. Still, the tie to Julian was entirely too close for comfort.

Her betrothed arrived just then, striding into the room with a ready smile that faded as his gaze met hers. "Meredith, what's wrong?"

No reason for obfuscation. "I am apparently being investigated by Bow Street. Did you know?"

Nothing changed in his face, but her heart sank.

"Let us say I am not surprised," he allowed, coming to her side. Fortune scampered out of hiding to weave her way around his boots.

She wanted to take comfort in the fact. Always she had trusted her pet's opinion of people more than her own. Still, his calm rankled. If she was outraged, why wasn't he?

"And you did not think to warn me?" she demanded.

"I hoped good sense would prevail, and I wouldn't have to warn you." He took her hand and drew her over to the sofa. "I will speak to Bow Street."

"Speak to Sir Alexander as well, then," Meredith told him, reluctantly sitting beside him. "He is the one directing this investigation."

Fortune jumped up between them and set about her own investigation, of which lap she would prefer.

"And his investigation will find nothing and thus assure him of your innocence," Julian countered. "You have nothing to fear from him, Meredith."

"Don't I?" She couldn't help her shiver. "You weren't there when he accused me of murder."

His hand tightened on hers. "I wish I had been. I would have defended your good name."

"Will you defend it now, should Sir Alexander bring charges?"

Julian frowned. "Charges of what?"

Meredith pulled away from him and threw up her hands, causing Fortune to jump down and stalk off behind the sofa in high dudgeon. "Who knows? Embezzlement? Attempted murder?"

Now his brows shot up. "Attempted murder? Of whom?"

"Of the gentlemen my ladies married," she replied. "This Bow Street Runner is asking questions of their households as well, probing into marriage settlements and wills, as if each lady intended her husband ill."

Julian shook his head. "Ridiculous. I've attended many of the weddings. Utterly besotted, the lot of them."

"Except perhaps Ivy and Lord Kendall," Meredith allowed. "Theirs is a marriage of convenience."

Julian leaned back. "Is that so? Small wonder Lord Kendall seemed so nervous that day. But the former Miss Bateman was ever a kind, generous soul. You couldn't make me believe she married him intending him harm."

"Sir Alexander doesn't need to convince you," she insisted. "He only needs to convince a magistrate, or, worse, Lord Kendall."

Julian rose. "Point made. Leave this to me. I'll speak to Alex."

Meredith stood as well. "You think a conversation will suffice?"

"I certainly hope so."

She could not be so optimistic. "I wish I could share your hope. I know what Sir Alexander's support has meant to you, Julian. But I very much fear, in the end, that you will have to choose between him, and me."

Travis delivered Meredith's invitation, a letter from Charlotte, two letters from Tuny, and a note from Miss Thorn the next day in Ivy's suite.

"Where did you find them?" she asked with relief.

His square-jawed face was pale. "They had been placed among his lordship's things, your ladyship. I don't think he even noticed. And I have had words with the footman who misplaced them. You will have no further trouble."

She thanked him and hurried to respond to the invitation, hesitating only a moment before confirming her and Kendall. Surely he would want to attend as well.

Charlotte's letter was full of news about the family. Daisy was bent on pursuing Sir William, who was proving difficult to bring up to scratch. Tuny had brought home a puppy to keep Rufus company. Both her sisters were eager to come visit when the Season ended. Tuny's letters extoled the virtues of Rex, her new puppy, who was nearly as clever as Rufus and might grow even bigger. And she certainly had room for a chicken or two, if Lord Kendall would be willing.

But Miss Thorn's note gave Ivy the most pause.

A Bow Street Runner has visited my clients, she'd written. *Though I do not consider you as such, he may. I do not know how Lord Kendall will react if the fellow approaches him.*

Neither did Ivy.

Since his impetuous kiss, Kendall had been more attentive—taking Ivy on longer walks in the summer sun, spending a greater amount of time with her and Sophia. She had hoped they were growing closer. Would questions from this investigator prove the lever that forced them apart?

"Will you inform me if Lord Kendall has a visit by a stranger?" she asked Travis when he came to collect her replies to the correspondence.

The tall footman did not so much as blink. "At once, your ladyship."

She could not doubt him.

Nor could she doubt Kendall's intentions when she stated her plan to return the dowager duchess' visit and he indicated a desire to accompany them.

She should have known he would take every precaution in traveling the two hours to the duke's estate on the River Thames. He brought out the largest of his carriages, the great lumbering travel landau in which they'd ridden from London, and filled it so full of pillows and blankets that there was barely room for him, Ivy, and the baby. He posted the coachman and head groom on the driving bench and stationed Travis at the back, with a brace of outriders in front and behind. A trunk on the top held extra clothes, toys, and food for Sophia.

And their riding comfort wasn't the least of it. He insisted on bundling the baby in so many pieces that Sophia lay stiff in her crib, unable to bend her arms and legs. She peered up at Ivy, little face tight and beginning to turn red, but from heat or frustration, Ivy wasn't certain.

"It is a warm summer day," Ivy reminded him. "You don't intend to dress to explore the arctic, do you?"

"No," he admitted with a frown.

"Then neither should Sophia." Ivy set about stripping the ermine-lined coat and wool gown from the baby.

Kendall's hands twitched as if some part of him longed to replace the coat on Sophia's little body, but he didn't stop Ivy from changing the baby into a long cotton summer frock and soft cloth bonnet, and they headed for the waiting coach.

Despite the fact that Kendall flinched at every bump and threw out his hands as if certain Sophia was about to tumble out of Ivy's grip, they reached the Thames safely and rolled over the bridge onto the island that held the duke's home.

A castle, she'd been told. It certainly reminded Ivy of one. Stone walls towered as high as three stories above the crest on which the house was situated, narrow windows looking toward the gleaming river in the distance. The walls encircled a cobbled courtyard, with the house wrapping around three sides. Footmen ushered them inside and up a flight of stairs to a room where they could remove their outer travel garments and wash their face and hands before being escorted to a room done in delicate pink, from the medallions on the silk wall coverings to the upholstery on the gilded furniture. Matthew would have hated the feminine décor. Kendall merely smiled.

The duke's family seemed well used to the space. Her Grace was seated on a high-backed chair that resembled nothing so much as a throne, His Grace and Jane were seated on one of the two flanking sofas, hands clasped in a way Ivy could only envy. The duke stood until Ivy was seated. His three daughters waited on the other sofa. No one had tried to smother them in winter clothes. They wore cambric, pretty gowns that left room to move, to play. Ivy caught Kendall eyeing them. If she knew her husband, Sophia was about to get a new wardrobe.

"How nice to see you, Lord Kendall, Lady Kendall," Her Grace the dowager said, waving them into chairs to the side of the group as her son returned to his seat.

"And Lady Sophia as well," His Grace put in with a smile to the baby.

Sophia cuddled closer to Ivy and glanced around at all the strangers.

Jane rose from the sofa, rubbing her hands together. "Right. We're glad you could join us. You are just in time for a science lesson."

Ivy thought either the duke or the dowager duchess would protest, or at least politely steer her away from the idea, but His Grace leaned back with a grin as if he couldn't wait to see what his wife had planned, and Her Grace smiled encouragement.

Jane looked to her girls. Larissa sat taller, Callie's eyes widened, and Belle wiggled in her seat. "Here is the question of the day. Does a thing change if it disappears from view?"

Kendall frowned as if he wasn't sure why she was asking such a question.

Lady Larissa frowned as well. "Certainly not. Just because *we* look away doesn't mean we have any effect on the object."

Kendall nodded agreement. Sophia sucked her thumb, as if considering the matter.

"Sure, are you?" Jane challenged. "Let's test that." She turned away from them, put her hands over her eyes, and began counting. "One, two…"

Larissa and Callie grinned at each other, slid from the sofa, and scampered from the room. Kendall gazed after them as if trying to make sense of it all.

Belle climbed down and came to take Ivy's hand. "Come with me, Lady Kendall," she whispered. "I know the best places to hide."

The dowager duchess waved a hand and settled herself in her chair as if prepared to watch the fun. Kendall followed Ivy. Very likely he wasn't about to let Sophia out of his sight.

Together they accompanied Belle along the silk-draped corridor.

"She's very good," the little blonde warned, "so you have to hide and be very, very quiet, even you, Lady Sophia."

Sophia's blue eyes were wide.

"Should we be playing?" Kendall murmured to Ivy with a look to his daughter.

"Absolutely," Ivy assured him. "It's never too early to start learning how to play well with others."

Belle pointed to a suit of armor standing in a niche. "That's a good place. She didn't find me there last time."

Still Kendall hesitated.

"Go on," Belle urged. "There's room. She'll finish counting soon."

As if to prove it, a loud voice came from the withdrawing room. "Ten!"

Belle ran to duck behind the long curtains on the window at the end of the corridor, leather slippers sticking out in plain sight. Ivy grabbed Kendall's hand and pulled him behind the armor, hunkering down as best she could with Sophia in her arms. The space would be wide for a six-year-old girl in hiding. Two adults and a baby made for cramped quarters. Kendall had to wrap his arms around her and Sophia. His sable hair brushed her temple, his breath caressed her cheek.

And suddenly it was very hard to breathe.

Jane strode out of the withdrawing room, hands on her hips.

"Now, where could they be?" she asked the corridor stretching out in front of her. "Look out, my lovelies. You know I hate to lose."

From the end of the corridor came Belle's bright giggle. Sophia wiggled as if trying to see where the sound was coming from, and the armor rattled as she brushed it.

Jane's eyes narrowed, and she stalked closer. Kendall obviously didn't like to lose either, for his arms tightened until he and Ivy were pressed together, his body warming her through her muslin gown. It was all she could do to keep hold of Sophia as her limbs felt liquid.

Jane made a show of looking all around, and Sophia's little head turned as she watched.

"Home free!" Callie's voice echoed from the withdrawing room.

"Oh!" Jane stomped her foot. "There's one. Now, where are the rest of them?" She glanced right, left, deep into the niche. Ivy clung to Kendall.

"Here I am!" Belle cried, popping out of hiding.

Jane hurried along the corridor to meet her, and Ivy drew in a breath.

"Stay quiet," Kendall murmured, as if their lives depended on Jane not finding them.

She would not have called out for the world. Even

Sophia cuddled close once more.

Larissa materialized from the stairwell. "You are supposed to make her find you, Belle."

"I know," Belle said, secure in Jane's embrace. "I just didn't want her to be disappointed. I can tell you where Lord and Lady Kendall are, if you like."

Jane laughed and led them back toward the withdrawing room. "I have a feeling Lord and Lady Kendall don't want to be disturbed." She winked at the armor as she passed.

Kendall climbed out of hiding, face flushed, then turned to help Ivy and Sophia as well. "Interesting game."

Did his lordship sound the least bit breathless?

"Very," Ivy said and hoped she didn't sound breathless as well.

They all returned to their seats. Jane settled in next to His Grace, who slipped an arm about her shoulders. But Larissa wasn't finished with their lesson.

"I was right," she said from her spot on the sofa beside Callie. "You didn't see us, but nothing changed."

"True," Jane allowed, head resting on her husband's arm. "But there's one other person still in hiding, and I imagine a few things will change when that person comes out."

Belle frowned. "Who?"

"I'm not sure," Jane said. "But about Christmas time, you will be joined by a baby even smaller than Lady Sophia."

The three girls stared at her.

"You will shortly have a brother or a sister," His Grace explained.

Ivy's heart leaped. "Oh, congratulations!"

He smiled at his wife.

Belle was still frowning. "Where is the baby coming from?"

Callie pointed to Jane. "Mrs. Winters said babies come from inside their mothers."

Belle looked thoroughly shocked.

Larissa's face tightened. "The baby will be yours. Not

like us."

His Grace stiffened, and Callie's face puckered.

"You are all my children," Jane assured her. "I will love this baby as much as I love you—no more, no less."

Larissa didn't look convinced. Concern was gathering on His Grace's face, and Kendall shifted as if uncomfortable with the entire conversation.

Ivy cleared her throat, and all eyes turned to her. "Sophia is not my baby. But I love her with all my heart. Nothing and no one could change that."

Beside her, Kendall put a hand over hers. She wanted to close her eyes and live in the touch.

Jane nodded. "You all know I loved my Jimmy. But I love your father and you as much. That's the wonderful thing about love. It only grows."

Larissa came and hugged her then, and so did Callie and Belle. The dowager went to wrap her arms as far as they would go around the five of them. Sophia put out both hands as if she wanted to join in too.

Kendall's face was stiff, his smile formal. Ivy would only hope this display would help him realize his heart was large enough to accommodate more.

Especially her.

CHAPTER EIGHTEEN

How easily they loved.

Kendall couldn't quite accustom himself to it. His father had done what he could with his two sons, and Nurse Wilman and their tutors had been encouraging, for the most part. Adelaide had filled a hole in his heart with her bright smiles and quick conversation. But no one he knew smiled and hugged and just seemed so very happy to be together.

Except Ivy.

He found it hard to leave her side when His Grace requested a moment of his time to review the plans for the weir.

"She'll be fine," Ivy whispered when he hesitated, and he could not tell her that it wasn't Sophia for once who had given him pause. He excused himself and followed the duke from the room, leaving the ladies to visit.

His Grace was tall and slender, sharp of mind and word. For as long as Kendall had known him, he'd held his power in a velvet grip. Now there was a new surety about him, a man who knew who he was and what he was meant to do.

"Allow me to add my congratulations to Lady Kendall's," he said as they descended to the ground floor.

The duke's smile was warm and wistful. "Thank you. I've never been particularly good about waiting for Christmas, but this time it will be all the more difficult."

Very likely. He'd waited for Sophia's birth with anticipation, only to lose Adelaide in the process. Then again, His Grace had lost his first wife on the birth of little Belle. Would he be the one person who could understand Kendall's dilemma?

He made himself focus as they went over the plans spread out on the table in His Grace's massive library. Kendall was glad to offer his support. As they straightened, he cleared his throat. "I wonder, would you be willing to discuss a personal matter?"

It was a gamble. Though they had lived in the same area all their lives, he was five years the duke's junior. They had attended the same school, but in different classes. They shared only a desire to protect and prosper the holdings they had been bequeathed and those who depended on them.

Perhaps it was that newfound surety that made the duke incline his head. "Certainly. How might I be of assistance?"

Kendall drew in a breath. "Like me, you lost a wife in childbirth. How did you move on?"

He eyed Kendall a moment. "In truth, I didn't. I left my daughters in the care of their grandmother, devoted myself to my responsibilities, certain that was my role as their father. Jane showed me fatherhood could be so much more."

Kendall nodded. "Yes, Ivy is showing me the same thing." His smile was slipping despite his best efforts. "But in marrying your Jane, did you feel no guilt in leaving behind the memory of your first wife?"

He spread his hands. "She left me behind, through no fault of her own. Evangeline would want her daughters well cared for."

"And their father?" Kendall pressed. "There is such a thing as mourning."

The duke's lean face softened. "Ah, you forget. Evangeline had been gone six years before I met Jane. It's been less than a year for you."

"So you think, with time, these feelings of betrayal will ease?"

He lay a hand on Kendall's shoulder, grounding him to the carpet. "Betrayal is a hard word. Did your wife love you?"

"Absolutely," Kendall said. "Without question."

The duke peered into his face. "Then wouldn't she want you to be happy?"

He should be able to answer that question with equal certainty, but he hesitated. In truth, there had been moments when Adelaide had been absorbed with her own happiness. He hadn't blamed her. She had been a sickly child, according to her parents, so moments of joy were something to grasp, to cling to. If his own happiness was sometimes forfeit, that had been a small price to pay to see her smile.

But did it follow that his own happiness must always be forfeit now?

"You give me much to consider," Kendall said. "Thank you."

The duke pulled back his hand. "Life has enough sorrow, Kendall. Take the joy when it is offered, and don't question it. I nearly lost Jane by doubting her. Don't make that mistake. If you care about Ivy, honor her as your wife, and let the past go."

The Season ended July thirtieth with the closure of Parliament. In anticipation, Daisy had written Ivy about the upcoming house party. Ivy had been firm in her refusal, going so far as to include one of the cards Mrs. Sheppard had ordered her, labeled Ivy, Marchioness of Kendall. She'd also written to Matthew to alert him to any schemes her

sister might try to force Ivy's hand. Only Petunia had
written back, meaning Daisy was having a fit of pique. Ivy
couldn't mind. She had enough to concern her without
worrying over her volatile sister.

For one thing, Sophia had come down with the sniffles.
Of course, Doctor Penrose had been summoned on the
first sneeze. He had examined her and prescribed rest and
plenty of liquids. That hadn't stopped Kendall from having
a cot installed in the nursery so he could be on hand should
Sophia need him day or night. If concern over the baby's
labored breathing hadn't kept Ivy awake, the thought of
Kendall sleeping just next door would have.

Then there were the preparations for the wedding. She
and Mrs. Sheppard had devised a plan to bake the cakes
and biscuits two days before the reception, then transport
them by the landau to the duke's estate. But that meant
coordinating Sophia's care with the baking and the use of
the landau with Kendall's expectations for their travel to
the wedding, without alerting him to her baking.

And then Tuny arrived.

Though her littlest sister had Ivy's blond hair and brown
eyes, she shared Daisy's more cynical nature. Ivy blamed
Mrs. Bateman. Their stepmother had taken a liking to
Tuny, who had been about Sophia's age when their father
had remarried. The new bride had loved billing and
cooing over the baby, handing Petunia to Ivy or Daisy
for changing and feeding and dealing with new teeth
and trouble sleeping through the night. Only when Tuny
had developed opinions of her own had their stepmother
begun giving her chores and treating her worse than a
servant, like her older sisters.

Ivy smiled as Tuny climbed down from the carriage
Kendall had sent for her sister and stared up at the great
house.

"It's like a cake with white icing," she marveled before
turning her gaze to Ivy's. "We should bake one while I'm

here."

Ivy glanced quickly to Kendall, who had come out with her to greet her sister. Dark circles wreathed his eyes, and his beard was just a bit on the rough side. But he interpreted Tuny's remark as Ivy had hoped he would.

"We have a talented baker on staff," he told Petunia as they started for the door. "I'm sure she'd be delighted to make whatever you like."

"Once the wedding is over," Ivy hurried to add. "We wouldn't want to overtax her."

Inside the entry hall, Tuny once more stopped to glance around. Then she whistled. "So many doors and stairs. How'd you remember what's where?"

Kendall bent to put his head on a level with hers. "You see that fellow?" he asked with a nod to Travis by the door. "You'll find him or someone like him sprinkled about. Ask one where you want to go, and he'll take you right to it."

Tuny stuck out her lower lip as if impressed. "All Miss Thorn has is a butler."

"And we have a housekeeper," Ivy said, nodding to Mrs. Sheppard, who came forward.

"Welcome to Villa Romanesque, Miss Bateman," she said.

Tuny giggled. "I'm not Miss Bateman. That's Daisy's name now that Ivy's married."

"You are every bit as important here as your sisters," the housekeeper assured her.

And that was all it took for Petunia and the housekeeper to become friends. Tuny had Travis and Mrs. Grunion in her pocket almost as quickly. She even won a smile from Percy, who had been given responsibility for helping her dress while she was visiting.

"I don't know how you do it," Ivy told her when they descended the stairs for dinner that night. Petunia had been put in the room down the corridor from hers and Sophia's. "It took me weeks to feel as if they were comfortable with me."

"You just have to be nice," Tuny said, hem of her muslin frock bouncing on the stairs.

"I'm nice," Ivy protested.

Tuny considered that a moment, brow furrowing. "You're quiet nice," she finally said. "I'm more loud nice. Sometimes that helps."

It certainly did. Kendall seemed pleased to have her with them, but then he had always gotten along with Tuny. Ivy didn't want to envy the way her sister made him smile at the dinner table that night.

"Sophia was much improved when I looked in on her before dinner," Ivy ventured when the conversation lulled.

The smile he gave her was worth the wait. "Doctor Penrose said she should be back to her usual self by tomorrow," he agreed.

"I can't wait to meet her," Petunia said.

His smile tightened just the slightest. "When we know she is well. We wouldn't want you to come down sick."

"I'm never sick," Petunia bragged. "Ivy takes too good care of us. Or else, she did before she came here. Now we have Charlotte." She heaved a sigh. "I love Charlotte, but she has no idea how to make cinnamon buns."

"More mashed potatoes, Tuny?" Ivy asked, motioning to Travis to serve her sister. She purposely ignored the curious look on Kendall's handsome face.

It wasn't until they were heading for bed that she finally had a moment alone with her sister. They were both in their long flannel nightgowns, and Ivy had dismissed Percy for the night. She knew Kendall was with Sophia, so she kept her voice low.

"I must ask you not to talk about my baking in front of Lord Kendall," she told her sister.

Tuny frowned. "Why? It's not a shameful thing."

"In his world, it is. Ladies don't dirty their hands."

"Why? Do they wear gloves?"

Her sister was ever the literal one. "No, Tuny," Ivy explained. "They don't go anywhere near the kitchen. No cooking, no baking. They have servants—dozens of servants—to do it for them."

"What if the lady's a better cook than they are?" Tuny challenged.

"She learns to hide her talents," Ivy said. "Mrs. Sheppard, Mrs. Grunion, and I have an understanding. I use the kitchen to bake, and they keep it quiet."

Tuny slumped. "Oh, good. For a moment there, I thought you were telling me no more cinnamon buns. I've been waiting weeks!"

Ivy hugged her. "For you, always cinnamon buns. There will be some for breakfast. Just don't ascribe them to me in front of Lord Kendall or any of his friends."

Tun straightened, wrinkling her nose. "*Lord Kendall.* Didn't his parents give him any other name? Charlotte calls Matty Matthew."

Ivy blushed. "He prefers his family name, but you must call him *my lord* unless he gives you leave to do otherwise."

"More rules." Tuny sighed as she slipped from the bed. "I'll try to remember, Ivy, but I agree with Daisy. Sometimes it's more than a body can bear."

"You are clever and determined," Ivy said as her sister headed for the door. "I have faith in you. Sleep well."

"You too."

As soon as her sister was out the door, Ivy wrapped her dressing gown about her, tiptoed to the connecting door to the nursery, and eased it open.

A lamp had been left burning low. The warm glow bathed Sophia's little frame, peaceful in her crib. It illuminated the lean form of Kendall, sitting in the rocker, head back, hair disheveled, lips parted in sleep.

Her heart turned over.

Ivy moved silently into the room and picked up the blanket from his cot. Carefully, she draped it about his shoulders, covered his strong arms. She was tucking it around his slender waist when she glanced up to find him watching her.

Face inches from hers.

The light gleamed in his dark eyes, picked out the copper in his hair. She should explain, wish him goodnight.

Instead, she leaned forward and pressed her lips to his.

So sweet, so brief, yet the kiss sent a tremor through her. His hands bracketed her waist, held her gently as he returned her kiss. Her heart ached from the joy of it. She slipped onto his lap, allowed him to hold her. Just a moment. Just for now.

Together, they rocked, Kendall's arms around her, her head against his chest. The only sounds were the faint creak from the chair, Sophia's soft breath. Ivy didn't want to move.

As if he knew he couldn't keep her here all night, he released her and helped her rise. His gaze avoided hers.

"Good night, Ivy. Sleep well."

Sleep? How could she sleep? She never wanted to leave his side.

But she wasn't really his wife. Not yet. His hesitation proved that.

She stepped back. "Good night, Kendall."

She made her way to her room, but it had never been harder to close the door.

Kendall sat in the rocker, staring at the glow of the lamp. Sophia murmured in her sleep and rolled over. He did not rush to check on her as he once would have. Ivy had taught him such movements were natural.

His growing feelings for Ivy felt natural too. When she'd pressed her lips to his, he'd wanted to hold her close, whisper praise in her ear. It had been pure indulgence to rock her in his arms so long. Would loving her truly be a betrayal of his love for Adelaide?

Sophia rolled over again, and he found two big blue eyes regarding him.

"Would you blame me one day for failing to honor your mother's memory?" he asked.

Sophia blinked, then blew bubbles at him.

With a smile Kendall went to pick up his daughter. He bobbed her up and down as he carried her to the rocker. "You're getting bigger all the time."

Because Ivy made sure of it.

Sophia lay her head against his chest, fingers lighting on the silver buttons of his waistcoat.

"Clever too," he told her.

Because Ivy was guiding her.

Everything good about his life now could be traced back to Ivy. Of course he would fall in love with her.

And yet…

At times he wasn't sure she was happy. Her usually sunny countenance would dim, a sigh breathe out. Surrounded by beauty and luxury, she was still restive. Why?

And then there was her baking. Petunia's slips had given Ivy ample opportunity to admit she was the baker. He had praised her work. She had to notice the number of buns and biscuits he consumed. Why not tell him the truth? Was his inability to love driving Ivy away?

He was still mulling over the idea and the possible solutions when their new man of affairs arrived the next day.

Mr. Dearborn was a heavy-set fellow with sandy hair curled around his ears and a tendency to mop his brow with decided frequency. Perhaps it was the journey in the hired coach. Travis had reported that the fellow had alighted sweating and trembling, as if the trip from London had been fraught with peril. Or perhaps Kendall's polite inquiries made him nervous.

"I have attempted to review your accounts in a certain amount of detail, my lord," he told Kendall, standing a few feet on the other side of the desk as if to assure Kendall he would never so much as dream of touching the polished surface. "Nothing too intrusive, of course. Sir Alexander has had you in excellent hands all these years. I would never intervene if it wasn't for your most express wish. It is your express wish, is it not?"

Kendall leaned back from the ledger the clerk had provided. "It is. Please continue. What did you learn on your review?"

"It is a vast estate," the fellow said, wiping his brow again. "Much larger than I realized on first inspection. And you have many investments that bear scrutiny. I believe I am coming to at least a partial grasp of the intricacies of income and expenditure. And as such I believe it wise, nay even prudent, to do nothing at this time. Wouldn't you agree, my lord?"

He almost began to miss Alex's plain speaking. "Let me be sure I understand you. You advise no changes to the estate or my investments at this time."

Dearborn scrubbed at his brow, handkerchief becoming limper with each movement. "Yes, my lord. It is only my opinion, of course. Moderation in all things. Haste makes waste. The man who rushes frequently falls. Don't you agree?"

Kendall kept his tone civil with difficulty. "And you find no irregularities in the accounts?"

He stepped back from the desk as if the mere thought was too distressing to contemplate. "Your investments are sound, dare I say cautious? My only concern—well, perhaps not a concern, you understand, but an item of note that might be somewhat telling…"

"Yes?" Kendall urged.

He visibly swallowed, and his voice came out shriller. "A

slight, a very slight, discrepancy in the household accounts. If you'd like, I could speak to your housekeeper about the matter."

Mrs. Sheppard would not suffer this fool gladly. "No need. If you would explain the discrepancy, I will bring it to her attention."

"A minor matter, of little significance in an account of your size, and yet, one must consider the lilies of the field, the hair of the sparrow, when keeping an accurate account. Don't you agree?"

"Quite," Kendall snapped. "Out with it."

Dearborn blinked. "Well, certainly, my lord. I have rarely been one to equivocate even in such trivial matters. Then again, perhaps no matter is truly trivial. There is more money expended than is accounted for in supplies, equipment, and wages. A minuscule amount compared to what has occurred in the past, truly, nothing to concern…"

"How much?" Kendall demanded.

"One hundred pounds in the last six weeks," he supplied. "Perhaps a little less, perhaps a little more. What man can truly count…"

"A man who hopes to manage my affairs," Kendall concluded, rising. "Thank you for coming out, Mr. Dearborn. I agree. We will make no changes at this time. I will expect you again next month. Safe journey back to London."

He attempted to transfer the fellow into Travis's capable hands, but his lead footman merely aimed his gaze over the top of Dearborn's flattening curls. "And the other gentleman who arrived with Mr. Dearborn, my lord?"

"What other gentleman?" Kendall asked, turning his gaze on the clerk.

His new man of affairs hunched in on himself. "I would not call him a gentleman, *per se*, my lord, though I certainly mean him no offense. He accompanied me for my protection."

There came the handkerchief again. Only since Ivy's arrival had Kendall begun to appreciate the trials of servants. Now he pitied the fellow's laundress. "And is there any reason for me to address your protector?"

"Oh, none, none," Dearborn warbled, but Travis took a step forward.

"I would be happy to address the fellow, my lord. He seems unusually interested in the estate, Lady Sophia, and Lady Kendall."

It was unlike Travis to interject, but Kendall saw his concern immediately. "Find him and bring him to me. Dearborn, you may wait in the entry hall."

"But my lord, there is no need…"

Kendall moved away from the whine, but not before he caught a look of satisfaction on Travis's usually impassive face. At least his head footman understood that, where Ivy and Sophia were concerned, Kendall would leave nothing to chance.

CHAPTER NINETEEN

Travis was swift in escorting the stranger to Kendall's study. By the crumpled collar on the man's worn wool coat, their visitor had resisted a little. Now he stood before Kendall, cap in hand but head high and gaze surprisingly assessing. There was something familiar about him, but Kendall couldn't place it.

"And what is your business on my estate?" Kendall asked.

"Just keeping busy while I wait for Mr. Dearborn, my lord," the fellow answered.

Standing by the wall, Travis shook his head ever so slightly, gaze on their unwelcome visitor.

"My staff seem concerned with the topics of your conversation," Kendall said, leaning back in his chair. "I do not appreciate gossip."

"Neither do I, my lord," he assured him. "Always one to look for the truth of the matter, in my friends, in my family. It's a trait you ought to practice."

"Here, now." Travis pushed away from the wall. "Keep a civil tongue in your head when you address his lordship."

The fellow bowed his head. "I meant no disrespect. If it would please his lordship, I'll just leave with Mr. Dearborn."

Perhaps that was for the best. Perhaps his conversation had merely been to while away the time. Kendall nodded agreement, and Travis came forward to take the man in hand. As their visitor slipped his tweed cap onto his head, recognition struck.

"Wait," Kendall ordered, climbing to his feet.

Both turned. Their visitor's gaze was nearly as wary as Travis's.

"You were at my wedding," Kendall accused him.

The fellow tipped his cap. "I was, my lord. At the request of a friend of yours."

That made no sense. What friend of his would send a rough lout like this to a wedding? Besides, he hadn't told most of his friends he was marrying again. He'd been out of touch with them since Adelaide's death.

"I'm afraid you'll have to do better than that," he told his visitor.

The man took a step closer under Travis's watchful eye. "I work for the Bow Street Magistrate's Office most days, but we're allowed to assist others from time to time. Your father had call to use my services."

So, this was the man his father had requested investigate the backgrounds of key new staff, business associates, sculptors. Who did the Runner think he was investigating now, and at whose request?

The realization was every bit as swift and twice as disturbing. Kendall came around his desk. "I give you leave to return to London but relay a message from me to Sir Alexander. If I confirm he sent you here to spy on Lady Kendall, I will discuss the matter with the Bow Street Office myself. Do I make myself clear?"

The Runner inclined his head. "Yes, my lord."

Kendall nodded, and Travis saw him out.

He returned to the desk. Was there no end to his former solicitor's arrogance? Was he so certain Ivy meant Kendall harm that he would go to such lengths?

Or was it truly the finances that concerned him?

He sat and pulled the ledger Dearborn had left closer. Now that the flaw had been pointed out to him, he saw it too. His expenses had been considerably higher when his father and Adelaide had been alive, yet they hadn't dipped all that much until about three months ago. That aligned with when he had gone to London for the Season, so perhaps his absence had brought about the change.

And yet, about the time Ivy had entered Villa Romanesque, there was a decided mismatch between what had been expended and what had been consumed.

He shook his head. This could have nothing to do with Ivy. She oversaw the household, but she had little to do with the accounting, as far as he knew. Why, she thought she had to economize.

He had plenty of funds. Even another one hundred pounds in the next six weeks would not seriously inconvenience him. But what if this was the opening salvo, a chance to see whether he would notice before the thief took more, a great deal more?

Only four people had access to the household accounts—himself, Ivy, Mrs. Sheppard, and his solicitor. If Sir Alex had been sticking a finger in the pie, he might stop now that Dearborn had pointed out the discrepancy, for surely the clerk discussed his activities with his employer.

Still, it might be time he found someone else to manage his affairs, whether Sir Alex liked it or not.

"She's coming!" Belle squealed as she ran toward Ivy, Petunia on her heels. Sophia in Ivy's arms reached out to grasp at them as they hurtled past, skirts flapping. Very likely the baby had never seen such movement.

Neither had the formal gardens at Villa Romanesque, Ivy was sure. Jane had brought her three daughters and the dowager duchess to visit. Petunia had showed them the chickens, then set up a game of catch-me-who-can. Larissa had attempted to be above such things, but when Petunia tagged her and pelted off, laughing, she'd joined in the fun as well. Now all four girls were weaving among the low hedges like swallows darting on the breeze, Jane in close pursuit.

"I'll catch you!" she warned, narrowly missing Callie as the girl vaulted a shrub, muslin skirts trailing.

"No, you won't," Larissa declared, seizing Petunia's hand and tugging her to safety.

"I hope Lord Kendall will allow Lady Sophia to join in when she's older," the dowager duchess said beside Ivy.

Ivy glanced at the baby in her arms. Sophia was bouncing up and down, tiny legs pressed against Ivy's belly, as if she couldn't wait. "I believe he will. She's getting stronger all the time."

"And that is to your credit, my dear," the dowager assured her. "There was every reason to fear she would follow her dear mother. More than one of us thought Lord Kendall would not be far behind."

Ivy stared at her as Belle and Callie ran past, intent on escape. "Was Lord Kendall ill too?"

The dowager pressed one hand to her chest. "Only in the heart. He and the first Lady Kendall were deeply in love, you know. I'm very glad to see he found he could love again."

Ivy kept her answering smile pleasant but refused to comment.

Indeed, what could she say? It had been two days since she'd kissed Kendall in the nursery, nearly two weeks since she'd attempted to dress her hair more elaborately, wear more stylish gowns. For all her hopes, nothing seemed to have changed. He remained friendly, thoughtful, but nothing more. What else could she do to convince him to make their marriage of convenience real?

"And how go the plans for this wedding?" the dowager asked, watching as her granddaughters veered off in three directions around the center fountain, their laughter carried on the warm air. Jane lunged forward and slapped her hand against Petunia's back, then dashed away before Ivy's sister could retaliate. Tuny's shoulders slumped for a moment, then she glanced around and ran after Belle, who was closest.

"Our baker is ready," Ivy promised the duchess, glad for the change in topic. "The biscuits and cakes will be delivered the afternoon before. I'm told your staff are prepared to receive and store them."

"Excellent." The dowager cocked her head. "I was hoping I might meet this paragon of bakers."

Ivy shifted Sophia between them. "Alas, she is enjoying some time away from her efforts. Perhaps when next you visit. How go the wedding plans on your end?"

"To your right, Petunia!" Larissa called, pointing her new friend toward Callie. Her sister scowled at her and barely dodged Petunia's reach.

"Well," the dowager replied, "it is small, as weddings go, no more than fifty or sixty people. We won't even need to open the larger hall. Still, it is a pleasure to have a wedding at the castle. My son is very fond of Miss Thorn's intended, Mr. Mayes. His late parents leased the estate next to ours along the river. A respectably family. Well thought of."

Her family was well thought of, particularly since Matthew had saved the life of the prince. Of course, there were always those who would look down on them for their humble beginnings. Was that why Kendall could not love her?

Mind still preoccupied, she only half attended to their visitors and her sister as they gathered in the emerald salon for refreshments a short time later. No, it could not be her family that held Kendall back. He had known who she was and had married her regardless of the gulf in their stations. Or was it her background that had drawn him to her? A more aristocratic lady might not have been willing to devote herself to Sophia.

Yet how could she lament her role? Every day the little

girl blossomed more. Only yesterday she had reached for Kendall and said, "Papa!" Ivy would never forget the joy and wonder on his face.

She glanced up now to find him in the doorway, gaze fond.

"Come join us, my lord," she called.

He came into the room with a nod all around. "I'd be delighted. I don't think I've ever heard my house so full of laughter."

"Do forgive us, my lord," the dowager said with a look to her granddaughters. "Frivolity does appear in our nature of late."

Larissa raised her head, and Callie hastily set down her biscuit and made her face more serious.

"No apology needed," he assured them, stopping beside Ivy's chair. "It is the sound of joy and nothing short of delightful."

"Then we should visit more often," Jane said with a grin.

He spread his hands. "You are always welcome, Your Grace."

"And you are welcome at the castle whenever it pleases you," Jane told him.

"And maybe someday Sophia will be big enough to play with us," Belle put in wistfully.

Kendall winked at Ivy before turning to the little girl. "Why, Sophia can play now. Shall I show you her favorite game? It involves a great brown bear."

Belle clapped her hands. "Yes, please!"

Would he really copy Matthew in front of the duchesses, no less? Jane was watching as eagerly as her daughters, though the dowager had a slight frown, as if she wasn't sure what he was about.

Kendall slid down onto all fours and growled. Sophia started giggling.

"She's laughing!" Callie cried.

"Laughing, is she?" Kendall asked, turning to thump up

to the towhead. "Do you laugh when confronted with a great brown bear?" He growled at her and snapped his teeth.

Callie reached out and patted his shoulder. "Nice bear."

"Me! Me!" Belle cried, and Kendall swung his head and ambled up to her.

She ruffled his hair, then leaned back. "Now go get Larissa."

Her older sister shook her head. "This is a game for babies."

"I always liked it," Petunia said. "I want to be a bear too." She hiked up her skirts and dropped to all fours. The dowager duchess' brows shot up.

But Ivy wouldn't have stopped her for the world. Petunia thumped along beside Kendall, bumping his shoulder from time to time, like two old friends out for a lark. Together, they advanced on Larissa, who narrowed her eyes at them.

"I am the queen of the bears," she announced. "And I command you to get her!" She thrust out her finger at her stepmother.

Kendall and Petunia obligingly turned to Jane, who pressed her hands to her cheeks. "Oh, no! Two bears! Whatever shall I do? Will no one help me?"

"I'll save you," Belle cried, darting between them. She shook her finger at Kendall and Petunia. "Bad bears! You go home."

Kendall and Petunia exchanged glances, then hung their heads and slumped back to Ivy's side. Sophia reached out and grabbed Petunia's hair, earning a wince from Ivy's little sister.

"There, there, poor bear," Ivy said, emboldening herself to stroke the sable of Kendall's hair. How soft, how thick.

He lay his head against her leg with a sigh.

"See what you've done?" Callie cried, hopping to her feet. "You made them sad."

"I'm sorry," Belle said, face puckering.

"It's just a game," Larissa reminded her. "They aren't really bears, and I doubt they're truly sad. Are you, Petunia and Lord Kendall?"

"No, of course not," Petunia said with a smile as she worked on removing Sophia's hold on her hair.

Kendall put a hand on Ivy's knee and gazed up at her. "How could any bear be sad at such kind treatment?"

How could she not hope when he looked at her that way?

Not long afterward, the dowager proclaimed it time to leave, and Travis sent for the carriages to be brought around. Kendall joined Ivy, Sophia, and Petunia on the drive to wave them off. The four of them had just turned for the house when one of the grooms raised the cry.

Another carriage was trundling up the drive.

"Are we expecting guests?" Ivy asked Kendall, lifting Sophia higher in her arms.

He shook his head. "Not that I've heard."

Petunia squinted as if trying to catch sight of a face in the window as the carriage turned up the rise. "Wouldn't be surprised if Daisy didn't decide to show up, neat as you please."

Surely Matthew would have written ahead. Ivy craned her neck, but she caught no glimpse of the passenger as the coachman drew the team up onto the flat and reined in, dust billowing. Sophia blinked and sneezed.

Travis ran out to lower the steps and open the door, then reached in a hand to help the occupant alight.

An older woman with greying hair poorly dyed a hideous red stepped down onto the gravel and gazed up at Villa Romanesque.

"Well, you've landed yourself in the money," she said as Ivy's stomach sank to her toes. "Come give your dear old mum a kiss."

Dear old mum? Ivy's mother had died birthing Petunia, just as Adelaide had died giving birth to Sophia. This could only be his bride's infamous stepmother, Mrs. Bateman.

Ivy had told Kendall about the woman, but he hadn't laid eyes on her the last time she'd visited the Batemans in London. He was a little surprised by her appearance— multicolored hair frizzed out around her face in a style more in keeping with his mother's generation, dress with a low cut and shiny fabric generally reserved for evening.

Shrugging her shawl closer, she clutched her beaded reticule and sashayed toward him.

"Don't stand there staring, boy," she told Kendall. "I've a trunk that needs to be carried."

Travis gulped back a gasp.

Ivy stepped forward. "Mrs. Bateman, we did not expect you. Allow me to introduce my husband, the Marquess of Kendall."

Kendall inclined his head. "Mrs. Bateman."

"I thought you went to Ireland," Petunia put in.

She yanked up on the shoulder of her satin gown, a garish green that clashed with her hair. "I was invited back to England. I had a duty to my girls." She beamed at Ivy and her sister. "And here they are, the darlings. And who's this little sweetheart?" She reached up two fingers as if to pinch Sophia's cheek.

Ivy reacted before Kendall could, thrusting the baby at him and away from her stepmother. "Kendall, would you see to Sophia? Petunia and I will deal with our visitor."

He pulled Sophia close but bent his head to Ivy's. "You're sure you don't need help?"

"I'll be fine," she assured him. "Just keep Sophia away from her."

He didn't like the sound of that. If the woman could not

be trusted near his daughter, he didn't much want her near Ivy either. But Mrs. Bateman was Ivy's relative, not his. He must abide by Ivy's wishes.

He took Sophia into the house, where Mrs. Sheppard was peering through one of the windows. She hastily stepped back. "A guest, my lord?"

"So it appears," Kendall said, handing Sophia to her. "Take Sophia to Becky, Mrs. Sheppard. Tell her to see that no one enters the nursery except our staff, Lady Kendall, or myself. If she has any trouble, have her call for Travis."

Mrs. Sheppard's eyes widened. "Is there a problem, my lord?"

"We are under siege," Kendall replied. "And I do not intend to give up without a fight."

Mrs. Sheppard curtsied and carried Sophia up the stairs just as Travis came through the door dragging an oversized trunk. It seemed Mrs. Bateman intended to stay awhile.

And she wanted to speak to him about the matter.

"Lord Kendall is a busy man," Ivy was telling her as they came through the door, Petunia just behind. "I will not have you disturb him."

"Oh, you-will-not-have-it," Mrs. Bateman sneered. "Marries above herself and puts on airs. Typical. Well, I have a promise to keep, and I'm going nowhere until I keep it."

Kendall strode up to them. "What do you need of me, madam?"

"Nothing," Ivy answered for her stepmother, moving between him and the woman. Petunia sidled around behind them and made for his side.

To Kendall's astonishment, Mrs. Bateman thrust out an arm and swept Ivy out of the way. "I'll speak my piece."

Kendall didn't wait to hear it. He caught Ivy as she swayed, held her gently.

"I'm so sorry," she whispered.

He had never seen such misery on her face. It wrapped

around his heart, urged him to act. He righted her. "No need to apologize, my dear."

"If you're finished billing and cooing," Mrs. Bateman said, foot tapping against the marble, "I'm waiting."

Kendall turned to her slowly, fire licking up him. Petunia shook her head at him, as if warning him.

"You may speak your piece, madam," he told her. "But if you think you can march into my home, lay hands on my wife, you had better reconsider."

She cocked a smile. "Oh, you're feistier than I was told. Makes no never mind. Just you remember one thing. I'm primary evidence."

Kendall frowned. "Evidence of what?"

"Of what you married into," she said. "I raised these girls, taught them all they needed to know about wringing the most from life and men like you."

Now Ivy gasped. "I never followed your advice."

"No?" she challenged. "What's this I hear about being trapped alone together?"

Ivy blanched.

"It was Daisy's fault," Petunia blurted out. "Ivy didn't know anything about it." She looked to her sister, face pinched. "Sorry, Ivy. I wheedled the truth out of Daisy after you left."

So, that was how the candelabra had come to be wedged into the latches. He could hardly blame Ivy for that. Her sister had ever been the more impetuous one.

"It's all right, Tuny," Ivy murmured. "Forgive me for not telling you, Kendall. I didn't think anything good could come of it."

"Why are you apologizing?" her stepmother demanded. "You caught yourself a nice rich lord, didn't you?" She turned to Kendall. "Just see that you remember one thing, my lord. The apple doesn't fall far from the tree."

And she threw back her head and cackled.

CHAPTER TWENTY

Ivy wanted the marble floor to crack open and swallow her whole. Either that, or the Romans who had once lived here to return, capture her horrid stepmother, and carry her off. Of course, the damage was already done. How could Kendall help but think the worst of Ivy and Petunia after seeing the woman who claimed to have raised them?

Kendall turned to Ivy, face once more the solemn mask she had not seen since London. "Ivy, do you wish this person in our home?"

Mrs. Bateman's face turned sorrowful. "Of course she does. She's the kind, merciful sort. Never could beat it out of her. You might keep that in mind. She requires a firm hand."

He stiffened, but he kept his gaze on Ivy. Waiting. Willing to put up with the slurs and cruelty if having this woman near somehow pleased Ivy. Willing to sacrifice, for Ivy.

No one but Matthew had ever sacrificed for her. Her father, her sisters, Mrs. Bateman—all of them expected Ivy to do what they expected of her. Good old Ivy, never an opinion of her own, never a place of her own.

Until him.

Ivy met his gaze. "No, I don't want her anywhere near me. She's done everything she could to hurt me and my sisters. I won't subject you and Sophia to her bile."

Mrs. Bateman gaped.

"Travis," Kendall barked, and the head footman dropped the trunk and surged forward far faster than dignity required. "Have the barouche brought around and escort Mrs. Bateman to the coaching inn at Walton-on-Thames. She can catch the mail coach to London from there."

"At once, my lord," Travis said, hurrying out the door.

Ivy's stepmother drew herself up. "You can't throw me out. What would your neighbors say, casting an old woman into the cold?"

That was one of her favorite gambits when all else failed. Play on the guilt, on the duty Society would say Ivy's family owed her. Ivy believed in turning the other cheek, but she had to consider Kendall and Sophia. Besides, Mrs. Bateman had already attempted to kidnap Petunia once. What if she tried again, and Ivy was too busy to prevent it?

"How I manage my estate is no affair of my neighbors," Kendall informed her stepmother. He turned to Petunia. "Miss Bateman, would you be so good as to check on Sophia for me?"

Tuny glanced between them, even more torn than Ivy in her loyalties. She still remembered moments when their stepmother had treated her kindly. Mrs. Bateman reached out a hand as if to stop her from leaving. No. Not this time. Not again.

Ivy placed herself between them. "Go, Tuny."

Tuny ran up the stairs.

Mrs. Bateman shoved Ivy away from her. "Wretch. You know I love that girl. You've no right to keep her from me."

Kendall stepped between Ivy and her stepmother, face flushed and hard. "Ivy has every right to determine what happens in our home. Moreover, madam, I am the local magistrate, giving me jurisdiction in this county. I will remind you that striking a member of the aristocracy is a crime punishable by death. Do not try me, for I will gladly see you up on charges."

"You wouldn't dare," Mrs. Bateman blustered, but she moved away from Ivy.

Kendall slid an arm about Ivy's waist, offering support. "Oh, madam, you might be surprised what I would do to protect my family. Ivy and I are in complete agreement there."

Ivy leaned against him, drawing strength from his. "Yes, we are."

"But I'm your mother," the woman all but whined. "I was there when your father passed. I gave you a home."

"You made me a servant in my own home," Ivy countered. For so long, she had said nothing, done her duty. It was time her stepmother heard the truth. "You belittled us, threatened us. I hoped that one day, you might realize that we were the best daughters you might have asked for."

"Best daughters," she sneered. "You were a disappointment then and now. Look what you've been given, and you can't even share."

She took the last ounce of guilt and threw it away. "I regret, Mrs. Bateman, that you cannot find it in you to be pleasant, but after the past we have shared, I will bear no responsibility for your future."

She thought her stepmother would argue. She had never listened to anything Ivy had said before. But Mrs. Bateman stuck her nose in the air.

"Fine. I knew this would be a waste of time. I told that solicitor he was barking at the wrong tree. It doesn't matter what he thinks of that Miss Thorn and her ladies. I knew your pretty face and winsome ways would win over the marquess."

Miss Thorn? This had to be why she had warned Ivy!

Kendall must have heard something of equal interest, for he stilled beside her. "Solicitor? What solicitor?"

Mrs. Bateman's smile turned crafty. "Oh, now I have

something you want. Well, it will cost you."

Ivy drew herself up, but Kendall nodded thoughtfully. "Very likely. Perhaps we can come to terms after you've had a chance to rest."

He meant to allow her to stay after all? Ivy could only stare at him.

Mrs. Bateman grinned. "Don't mind if I do. Nice big room with a nice soft bed. And none of those winged babies on the ceiling. They're enough to give a woman nightmares."

"Villa Romanesque has any number of fine bedchambers," Kendall said. "And an equally fine cellar, equipped with iron doors that lock. I've never had call to hold anyone in the dark and damp, but I'd be willing to make an exception for you." His look hardened. "The name, madam!"

She flinched. "Prentice. Sir Alexander Prentice. The least you could do is pay for my room at the inn."

The jingle of tack and the thud of hooves outside told of the barouche arriving. Travis opened the door and stepped inside, holding it ready for Mrs. Bateman.

"Pay the innkeeper for room and board for one night," Kendall instructed him. "And leave enough for the coach to London."

"My lord," he said with a steely-eyed glance at Mrs. Bateman. A groom hurried in to collect her trunk.

Ivy's stepmother draped her shawl more closely around her. "I'll go. But don't think you've seen the last of me."

"That is up to Ivy," Kendall said. "But if you ever arrive at my door again without her pre-approval, I will set the hounds on you."

She swallowed visibly, but she strutted out to the waiting carriage.

Kendall shut the door behind her.

"I thought you told Tuny you didn't have hounds," Ivy said as he turned to her.

"We don't," he said, returning to her side with a smile.

"But she doesn't need to know that."

Relief cast her into his arms. "Oh, Kendall, thank you! I've never had the courage to stand up to her before."

He held her a moment, then let her back with a smile. "I can see why you might find her daunting. She is rather good about wielding the knife."

"And twisting it." Ivy shuddered. "I hope you don't believe her."

Once more his face hardened. "About Sir Alex putting her up to this? I'm sad to say I do believe her. I doubt she would have returned to England on her own and confronted us this way. Who else has cause to wish us ill?"

Ivy swallowed. "And the message he wanted her to bring? That the apple doesn't fall far from the tree?"

He took her hand. "You are not an apple, Ivy. And you didn't fall from her tree. You are a woman of character who chooses every day to help those around her. Comparing you to her is like comparing fine china to a battered tin plate."

Her lips were trembling. "Then you don't think I tricked you into marriage, that I'm out for your money."

Something crossed his face, but he answered her readily enough. "Certainly not. You are Sophia's mother, the mistress of Villa Romanesque. I have complete faith in you."

Mother. Mistress of the house.

Not wife. Not love.

Some men would have believed their odious stepmother and thrown Ivy and Petunia out along with her. Kendall believed her. Yet her heart ached.

Never had she talked back to her stepmother before today. Never had she spoken a word against anyone. Never had she demanded more than what she had earned.

But she wanted more now. So much more. If she could be forthright with her stepmother, she owed Kendall no less.

"What if I want to be your wife?" she asked.

He released her and stepped back, and her heart cried out. She shouldn't have taken the chance. She shouldn't have pushed him. She should have given him more time.

But she wanted his love now. She needed his love now. Everything else felt so dull, so lifeless.

So empty.

He glanced around, and Ivy realized Mrs. Sheppard, Martha the elder, or one of any number of servants could appear at any moment. Though she knew they were well trained to ignore the conversations of their employers and guests, she truly didn't want them overhearing this particular discussion. Especially if Kendall meant to kindly refuse her. She wanted to bear that pain alone.

"Perhaps," he said, "we can continue this conversation at a more suitable time. I must go to London."

Ivy gathered her frayed dignity with difficulty. "London? Why?"

He glanced at the door as if wishing himself gone even now. "Sir Alexander made a fatal mistake. I will not allow anyone to harm those I love. It's time he was brought to realize that." He looked back at her. "Will you have dinner with me when I return tomorrow?"

"Of course," Ivy agreed, thoughts in a turmoil. She could not deny the wily solicitor had made a powerful enemy in Kendall, or that Sir Alex deserved censure for his behavior. And her stepmother's mention of Miss Thorn could only mean the solicitor's vengeance was broader than Ivy alone.

But her mind kept coming back to one word. Kendall had said he would now allow harm to those he *loved*.

Did he include Ivy in that number?

His valet was packing, his travel landau being readied.

Kendall had kissed Sophia farewell on the forehead and Ivy farewell on her hand. Now all that remained was to discuss matters with his housekeeper in his study.

And settle his thoughts for the coming battle.

So he stood gazing out the window at the fields stretching toward the River Blackmole, but the waving grain, the wall of trees, held no more appeal than this betrayal. From the first, his former solicitor had been against Ivy. Kendall knew the prejudice toward those who entered the aristocracy through marriage rather than birth. But Ivy had more than earned her place at his side.

He was the one lacking.

He was not one to make impassioned speeches before the House of Lords, to exhort his tenants to harder work. He was known for his polished demeanor, his quiet nature. Those traits may have conspired to make some question the capacity of his mind or the loyalty of his character. Both Sir Alex and Mrs. Bateman had assumed he'd believe the woman's tale that Ivy was some kind of schemer, that he couldn't see the gem he had married. Worse, they didn't realize he would protect his family. They must consider him a coward.

He could not argue there.

He was ready to face his own cowardice. He'd called it guilt; he'd called it love. He'd prided himself on protecting Sophia. Ivy had made him see his protection as overbearing control, a way to silence the fear inside him. The truth of the matter was that he had been so afraid of betraying his first wife he had nearly failed his second. That was inexcusable, and it ended now.

He loved Ivy. And she was right, as she so often was. Loving her did not mean he loved Adelaide and Sophia less. Thanks to Ivy's love, his heart had grown large enough for more.

His Grace the Duke of Wey had reminded him that happiness did not have to go to the grave. Kendall could believe that now. He wanted to be able to stand before his father, his mother, Adelaide, and God and tell them that he had continued to love.

A wonderful, amazing woman who was more than he would ever deserve.

Unlike Sir Alexander, he refused to allow his protection to erode into control.

Behind him, he heard the rustle of skirts. Turning, he found Mrs. Sheppard in the doorway. She dipped a curtsey. "My lord. You had need of me?"

"I do," he said, motioning her into the room. "You will have heard that I will be traveling to London this afternoon. I plan to return by mid-afternoon tomorrow."

She inclined her head. "Very good, my lord."

"I have two requests for dinner tomorrow night."

She nodded, waiting, but he could not miss the glint of curiosity in her eyes.

"First, I wish to dine alone with Lady Kendall in the pavement room. Travis may serve, but he is to withdraw immediately after each course."

If she found the request surprising, she was too well trained to show it. "I'll have the staff begin moving furniture immediately. And the second request?"

She would likely think him mad. He wasn't entirely sure she was wrong. But Ivy had done everything to make this house a home, to love Sophia and him, asking nothing in return until today. Then she had asked only what was her due. She wanted to be his wife.

The fact humbled and exalted him. He had to find a way to show her he cared, that he understood her needs, that he would make her his equal partner from this day forward.

He met Mrs. Sheppard's gaze. "Teach me to bake biscuits."

CHAPTER TWENTY-ONE

"And so we have a full complement for our wedding," Meredith concluded, setting down her list but keeping a hand on the parchment in her lap lest Fortune decided to attack it.

"Excellent," Julian said. He straightened one arm along the back of the sofa and rested it on Meredith's shoulder. "What remains to be done?"

She pulled her list closer again as a grey head appeared over the seat of the sofa, copper-colored eyes wide in their scrutiny. "Surprisingly little. The Earl of Carrolton insisted on furnishing flowers, the Marquess of Kendall's baker is creating the sweets for the breakfast afterward, Lydia and Charlotte helped me choose a gown, and Patience and Gussie are bringing a special perfume."

"Let me guess," he said with a tweak of the silk at her shoulder. "Lavender."

Meredith smiled. "Of course." Glancing up, she met his gaze and felt herself slipping into the depths. Julian leaned forward and brushed her lips with his. She felt as if he touched her heart as softly.

Something whipped past her skirts even as she heard Mr. Cowls clearing his throat. Julian straightened away from her, giving her a clear view to the doorway.

Where Lord Kendall waited, polite face turning pink, as Fortune wound around his boots in greeting.

"The Marquess of Kendall, madam," her butler intoned.

"Forgive the interruption," her visitor said, hesitating in the doorway. "I had hoped to ask you for Mr. Mayes's direction. As usual, you and Fortune anticipate my needs."

Fortune rubbed her head against his boot as if proud of the fact.

"You are always welcome, Lord Kendall," Meredith assured him. "Won't you join us?"

He paused only a moment more before coming into the room and taking a seat on the chair opposite them. Fortune hurried to follow. He took one look at the cat and jiggled his leg just the slightest, setting the tassel on his boot to swinging. Fortune crouched, watching.

"You were looking for me?" Julian ventured, both arms now at his sides, leaving Meredith feeling a bit empty.

Lord Kendall's leg stilled, and Fortune gathered her haunches under her. "I would like you to consider accepting me as a client."

That would be a coup. Besides His Grace the Duke of Wey, Lord Kendall would be Julian's most prestigious client. The influence of the two men combined could even earn him consideration for a baronetcy, one of his fondest wishes.

If Julian had come to the same realization, he gave no sign. "In what capacity?" he asked as if the request bore no more weight than conversation about the weather.

Lord Kendall didn't flinch as Fortune launched herself at his tassel. "Solicitor, man of affairs, the fellow who oversees all my holdings."

Julian's reddish brows went up at last. "I am honored, my lord, but I was under the impression you had such an agent. Sir Alexander Prentice, I believe."

Meredith willed herself not to stiffen at the name. Julian had assured her he would deal with the fellow, but she had not been made privy as to how or when. She had also heard no more of the Bow Street Runner and could only hope he had moved on to investigate real crimes.

Lord Kendall appeared to have as little liking for the solicitor, for his face hardened. "Sir Alexander has in every way made known he no longer wishes to be of service."

He'd made an enemy of Lord Kendall? Was the man mad?

Julian leaned back on the sofa as if he held as much doubt. "I cannot believe he would refuse you. He served your father."

Lord Kendall shifted. "May I speak candidly? Nothing I say must leave this room. I will not subject my wife to gossip."

Meredith raised her head. "I do not gossip, my lord."

His mouth quirked under his mustache. "I did not think you did, Miss Thorn."

"And neither do I," Julian assured him, brown eyes interested. "Even though we have no formal commitment as yet, I consider this discussion part of client privilege."

"Good." Lord Kendall moved his boot, setting Fortune darting back. "Sir Alexander has made it abundantly clear that he considers my wife beneath the dignity of a marchioness. He attempted to stop me from endowering her sisters, something I'd promised her in my proposal. And I have suspicions that he has been siphoning funds from the estate."

Meredith gasped. "The dastard!"

"These are disturbing allegations," Julian said with a frown. "I trust you have proof."

"Not enough to convince a magistrate," the marquess allowed, "but enough to give me pause about continuing with his services. He also attempted to introduce an unsavory person into my household, giving Ivy and her little sister a few bad moments. I am done with him."

Meredith put her hand on Julian's arm to stop him from responding. "Unsavory person? In the form of a Bow Street Runner, perhaps?"

Lord Kendall eyed her. "He visited you as well?"

"He imposed himself on many of my associates," Meredith informed him. "I trust you sent him packing."

Again, his mouth hinted of a smile. "I did, with a message to Sir Alexander, a message he did not heed, for he sent Mrs. Bateman to visit."

"The affrontery!" Meredith cried, stiffening. "Are Ivy and Petunia safe?"

Julian glanced between them. "Mrs. Bateman?"

"My wife's stepmother," Lord Kendall supplied.

"And a thoroughly unpleasant person," Meredith added. "You recall when Charlotte, Daisy, and Petunia stayed the night last month for their own safety."

Julian nodded.

"Do not be concerned on their behalf," Lord Kendall told her. "On my way here, I alerted Sir Matthew as to the woman's return to England. She will be dealt with. For now, I must deal with Sir Alexander."

That made one of them. Meredith glanced to Julian. Once more his face was composed, lean body still.

"I see," he said. "Before we continue, Lord Kendall, you should know that I mentored under Sir Alexander and have until lately considered him a friend."

Lord Kendall eyed him. Fortune chose that moment to dash out of hiding and pounce on his tassel again. Meredith moved to secure her pet.

"What changed your mind?" Lord Kendall asked Julian as she brought Fortune back to the sofa.

"I had conversations that troubled me," Julian admitted.

"Sir Alexander is not fond of me," Meredith put in.

"Indeed he is not," Kendall said. "Mrs. Bateman, my wife's stepmother, told us he hoped to ruin both you and Ivy."

Julian jerked to his feet. "You're certain?"

Lord Kendall spread his hands. "As certain as I can be given the woman's character."

Meredith could almost see the struggle in Julian. He wanted to believe her and Lord Kendall, but Sir Alexander was like a father to him, and Julian was used to dealing in subtleties, not absolutes.

He blew out a breath. "The only excuse I can think, and it is a poor one, is that Sir Alexander seeks to protect you and me. But he is mistaken about Meredith, and I believe him to be mistaken about Lady Kendall as well."

"Then you'll accept my commission?" Lord Kendall asked.

Julian held up a hand. "On one condition. We go see Alex together, ask him to explain himself. After years of association, it would seem he deserves as much."

Meredith wasn't so sure, but she decided not to question him. Julian too deserved to learn the truth. She stood. "Allow me a moment to settle Fortune, and I'll join you."

It was to Lord Kendall's credit that he did not look to Julian as if she needed his permission. "This will not be pleasant, Miss Thorn," he said, face once more solemn. "I would like to spare you."

"As would I," Julian assured her. "It seems you were right to be concerned about Alex. He has listened to none of our protests. I will give him one more chance. Either way, allow me to put a stop to his interference."

She could not remember that last time she'd had a champion. Now it seemed she had two. How easy to send them off to do battle for her, offering them her blessing with a wave of a handkerchief. But for too long she had lived under the specter of Sir Alexander's threats. It was time she ended this, for her, for Julian, and for her clients.

"Sir Alexander threatens not only me but any woman with whom I have associated," she told them both. "I will not have it. I'd prefer to tell him so myself."

Julian offered her his arm. "Then let us give Fortune to Cowls and put Alex in his place, once and for all."

Four clerks were busy copying papers as Kendall, Miss Thorn, and Mayes entered the offices of Sir Alexander. Dearborn was among them. He glanced up, washed white, popped to his feet, and hurried to meet them.

"Lord Kendall, Mr. Mayes, what a surprise, that is a pleasure, yes, most assuredly a pleasure, is it not? And the lady. Lady…Kendall?"

Dearborn had not met Ivy, so it was a logical conclusion. Indeed, Miss Thorn looked every inch the lady with her straw hat trimmed with curling ostrich plumes and her lavender velvet short jacket.

"Miss Thorn," she informed him in tones that dripped icicles. "We are here to see your master."

Dearborn bobbed like a bird on the waves, perspiration beginning to glisten along the edges of his sandy hair. "Certainly, that is he would be delighted, I suspect. Allow me to tell him you are here, if you'd be so kind."

"No need," Julian said, unlatching the short, wrought iron gate that separated the entryway from the clerk's area. "We'll only be a moment." He motioned Kendall and Miss Thorn ahead of him, and they started down the aisle between the cluttered desks, the other clerks stopping their work to stare.

Dearborn scurried along behind them. "Should I bring your books, Lord Kendall? Tea? Lemonade?"

"Nothing," Kendall assured him. "But gather up everything having to do with my holdings and finances and have them ready."

He glanced over at the clerk to find Dearborn's Adam's apple bobbing along with him. "Yes, my lord, at once, my lord, that is…"

Julian opened the door, then, and all Kendall's attention went to the man sitting in the high-backed armchair.

Sir Alex had been leaning back, feet out to the hearth, steaming cup at his elbow on the polished wood desk, as if all was right with the world.

Anger pushed Kendall forward, but he kept his face calm. Still, his former solicitor took one look and climbed to his feet. "Lord Kendall, Julian. Is there a problem?"

Julian shut the door on Dearborn and turned. "In truth, that's what we'd like to ask you. Lord Kendall, if you'd be so kind."

Kendall knew the moment the solicitor noticed Miss Thorn, for he stiffened, and his nostrils flared, as if he were a bull sighting an interloper in his field. Miss Thorn's head came up as if she was fully prepared to fight him. So was Kendall.

"I was paid a visit by a Mrs. Bateman," he said. "She claims you arranged for her to disturb my wife."

Alex spread his hands. "One cannot believe the claims of those of such low estate, my lord. I'd have thought you'd realize that by now."

"Do you dare compare that harridan with Lady Kendall?" Miss Thorn demanded.

Heat flamed up Kendall, and his fists balled at his sides.

Alex's lips barely lifted, making the look more sneer than smile. "How do you know I meant Lady Kendall?"

Now Miss Thorn's cheeks reddened. Kendall thought Mayes would take umbrage, but he moved into the room to lean a hip against the solicitor's desk. "And how did you know Mrs. Bateman was of low estate if you had never met?"

"Lady Kendall's maiden name was Bateman," Alex supplied, dropping his hands and returning to his chair without inviting any of them to sit. "I assumed the two were related."

"The same way you assumed Meredith was guilty of murder?"

Miss Thorn glanced to Julian in obvious surprise. So did

Kendall. His new solicitor's voice was a purr, but power simmered under it. For all his protestations, it seemed he had an equal reason to dislike Sir Alex.

The older solicitor gave no indication he heard the anger behind the words. "I cannot help that some men are blinded by a pretty face," he said. "That's why they hire me—to protect themselves from their own failings."

Miss Thorn drew herself up. "Failings, sir? Who do you think failed?"

He looked to Kendall as if expecting an answer. But marrying Ivy was no failure. What had started as an act of devotion to his daughter had become so much more. He could say with certainty that he was a better father, a better man, because of Ivy.

"If I have been failed," he said to the smug solicitor, "it is in not recognizing the worth of those around me. I would trust Ivy with my life. You, sirrah, are another matter."

Alex shrugged. "Which is why I transferred your affairs to Dearborn. Do you tell me he is inadequate to the task?"

"He certainly doesn't inspire confidence," Kendall replied. "But then, I suspect you knew that when you assigned him the role. Did you expect me to come running back?"

"I expected you to realize the folly of your decisions eventually," Alex said with maddening calm. "You will, you know. She isn't clever enough to hide her tracks, despite her mentor. Dearborn tells me you've already noticed irregularities in the household accounts, coinciding with the entry of your wife into your household."

Miss Thorn glanced Kendall's way.

"He made sure to bring them to my attention," Kendall told them. "But I was more interested in the earlier discrepancies, dating back to when my father was alive."

Sir Alex snorted. "Dear boy, there are no such discrepancies. I handled that effort myself."

"They weren't obvious until Dearborn went over the ledgers," Kendall acknowledged. "He attempted to correct the inaccuracies, which only made them all the more visible. Someone in your firm has been stealing from my accounts."

Miss Thorn's eyes narrowed, but Alex shook his head and turned to Julian. "You see? Blind. I can only hope your sight is clearer."

"Oh, it is," Julian answered. "Lord Kendall asked me to take over his holdings. I cautioned him to share his concerns with you first."

"Quite right," Alex said. "Between the two of us, we will set him straight."

Kendall drew himself up, but Julian spoke first.

"I think not. Lord Kendall is on a perfectly straight path already. So am I. I will always remember how you fostered my career, sir, and I have no proof of Lord Kendall's allegations about the discrepancies in his accounts, but I can no longer align myself with a man so arrogant he feels justified meddling in the affairs of others."

Miss Thorn went to put a hand on his arm.

Alex surged to his feet. "Meddling? I do not meddle, sir. Noble houses rise and fall at a word from me. Countries go to war."

"Keep your kings and countries," Kendall said. "I discharge you from my service. Turn over everything to Mayes today."

"If that is your wish," Alex said, voice haughty, "but do not think you can be done with me so easily."

Kendall took a step forward. "And do not think that because I prefer to remain polite I would allow you to do the least to any member of my family. If you say a word against Lady Kendall, I will see you up on charges of theft."

"If you dare bring me up on charges, I will countersue for defamation of character," Alex vowed. "And when I make my defense, I will be sure to bring Mrs. Bateman as a witness to the character of your wife and point out that the latest discrepancies came when Lady Kendall was given charge of the accounts. I will also share the lavish gifts your lowly bride demanded for the privilege of marrying you. And I will be certain to trace her avarice back to the woman who trained her."

His gaze speared to Miss Thorn, as if she was to blame for it all. She stood tall, proud.

"Do your worst," she spat out. "I am no longer afraid of you."

Alex's chuckle was as ugly as his sneer. "You should be."

Kendall had never been a man of violence, but he was sorely tempted to plant his fist in the solicitor's face.

"No," Julian said. "She should not. You will do nothing to hurt her."

Breath coming heavily, Kendall glanced his way. The younger solicitor's face was set, his stance firm on the carpet.

"Lord and Lady Kendall are now my clients," he said. "You will do nothing to cause them embarrassment or concern. Nor will you trouble Meredith Thorn or any of her clients."

"And what will you do?" Alex demanded. "Bring me up on some paltry offense? You know that's a double-edged sword. I can make the magistrates dance to my tune."

"I have seen you do it, to my sorrow," Mayes replied. He was smiling, but there was nothing pleasant about it. "No, I have another thought. You mentioned that wars start at a word from you, and here we are at war with America, after you ceased negotiations."

Was that a pallor creeping into the solicitor's face? "The Yanks are unreasonable," he blustered. "Everyone knows that."

"Not everyone," Miss Thorn said with a look of awe to her betrothed.

"While you were away," Mayes continued, "I was approached by Lord Hastings, who arranged for me to be introduced to His Royal Highness. How do you think

England's spymaster and the future king would take it if I mentioned my concerns about your conduct in America to them?"

Alex licked his lips. "My service speaks for itself."

"Yes," Mayes said, "I fear it might." He turned to his betrothed. "Are you satisfied with the outcome of our interview, my love?"

Her smile was all for him. "Indeed I am."

He turned to Kendall. "And you, my lord?"

Kendall looked to his former solicitor, who had sunk back into the chair, heavy body hunched and face ashen. He knew a beaten man when he saw him.

"Yes, Mr. Mayes," Kendall said. "I believe I am, and your services on my behalf are noted. You are hired at double the fee of my former firm, and I look forward to a long and prosperous association."

CHAPTER TWENTY-TWO

Kendall was away less than thirty-six hours, but each moment had dragged for Ivy. Sophia was fussy, and even Petunia's antics hadn't been enough to distract the little girl for long.

"Do you miss him too?" Ivy asked, walking the baby in her arms around the nursery.

Sophia sighed and rested her head on Ivy's shoulder.

Mrs. Sheppard herself came to let Ivy know when the coach arrived on the drive.

"His lordship will meet you for dinner," she explained, bustling into the room. "Becky and I will watch Lady Sophia, with Miss Bateman's kind help."

Petunia readily agreed, but the housekeeper wasn't finished. "Now, let's get you changed," she said to Ivy, striding for the door to Ivy's room.

Ivy didn't argue. In truth, she wanted to look her best. Kendall had said he intended to continue their conversation when he returned. She wanted to give him every encouragement to say yes to making their marriage real.

"The blue silk," Ivy told the housekeeper as Mrs. Sheppard headed for the wardrobe.

The older woman retrieved the gown just as Percy hurried into the room to help as well.

"And the gold sash," the maid said, pulling the satin

ribbon from the dressing table drawer. "As soon as you're dressed, your ladyship, I'll see to your hair." She smiled at Ivy.

Ivy smiled back.

A short while later, she stood gazing at herself in the Pier glass mirror. Her hair was piled up with curls lose about her cheeks, like spun gold. The fit of the gown called attention to her womanly curves. More, there was a confidence in her posture, a light in her eyes. For the first time, she thought she just might look like a marchioness.

"A bit of rouge?" Percy suggested, holding up the pot.

"No," Mrs. Sheppard said. "Her ladyship is perfect as she is."

Though she knew it spoiled the image she was trying so hard to cultivate, Ivy turned and hugged her. After a moment's hesitation, the housekeeper returned the gesture.

"His lordship requested dinner in the pavement room at six," Mrs. Sheppard said as she disengaged. "Give him a half hour, and then go to him."

Kendall climbed the stairs to his room. Amazing how much flour could get on a fellow, even when wearing one of the voluminous aprons of the kitchen staff. He had just enough time to change before meeting Ivy for dinner. Every minute seemed too long.

And yet, as he passed the room next to his, he felt as if someone called to him.

He stopped, stared at the door. It was time.

He opened it and stepped inside. Memories tiptoed toward him—Adelaide's gasp of delight when he'd given her his mother's jewels, the light in her weary eyes when she'd first held Sophia. He moved to the bed, ran a hand over the coverlet, cold and stiff from disuse.

"You will not be forgotten," he promised. "You are not being replaced. I will make sure Sophia knows all about the woman who gave her life to birth her. But it is past time I let you go."

He thought the room sighed in agreement. Heart lighter, he went to the jewelry box on the dressing table and retrieved what had always belonged to the Marchioness of Kendall. Then he left the room to change for dinner with his wife.

If the thirty-six hours were long, the next half hour was endless. Ivy didn't dare go to Sophia for fear of ruining her gown or hair. In the end, she wandered about the upper corridors, trying different approaches in her mind. She'd already told him she wanted to be his wife. What else could she say, what could she do, to convince him?

As she descended to the main floor, her heart was beating as fast as if she'd run the whole way, and her skin felt as if bees buzzed along it. She slipped into the pavement room, followed the path past the statues. At least they seemed to be smiling at her, even the two former Lady Kendalls.

The staff had erected a round table and two harp-backed chairs next to the pavement. The silver-edged china gleamed in the light streaming down from the high glass roof.

But the splendor was nothing to Kendall. He had dressed in a jacket of deep blue velvet, and a silver-shot waistcoat peeked out above and below. Once more his hair was perfectly combed, his mustache and beard neat. The glow in his eyes encouraged her closer.

They gazed at each other a moment, then Kendall hastened to pull out one of the chairs for her.

Ivy gathered her skirts and sat, and he helped her scoot

the chair forward. For a moment, with his arms bracketing her, as if she was in his embrace.

He took his seat across from her with a smile.

In the silence, she could hear the fountain playing.

"Did you accomplish what you'd hoped in London?" she asked.

"Yes, thank you," he replied, settling himself on the chair. "I discharged Sir Alex and his firm and hired Julian Mayes. You will not be troubled again."

He had gone to such effort, for her. "Thank you. I know he served you well for a long time."

He grimaced. "Perhaps not as well as I'd hoped. There are discrepancies in the household accounts."

Her hands were trembling. She folded them in her lap. "Discrepancies?"

"Funds expended with no supplies noted, that sort of thing. Clearly, he thought to cheat us."

Much as she loathed the solicitor, she could not allow him to take the blame. "It wasn't Sir Alex, Kendall. It was Mrs. Sheppard, I fear."

He frowned. "Mrs. Sheppard?"

"On my behalf," Ivy hurried to assure him. "I should have told you sooner, but I was afraid you would be disappointed in me." She swallowed and sat taller. "I am the new baker."

Kendall's brows went up, but before he could speak, Travis brought in the first course. Ivy couldn't bring the lovely mulligatawny soup to her mouth as she waited for Kendall's answer. He did not respond until the footman had left the room again.

"I know," he said, silver spoon in one hand. "That's why I asked Mrs. Sheppard to order you the best equipment. You are very good at baking, Ivy, and you clearly enjoy it. I would never insist that you stop."

"But it's not ladylike," Ivy protested.

He shrugged. "And marquesses are not known for

digging in the dirt, but my father and I did so gladly to unearth the pavement. Besides, many ladies have unique interests. Some garden when they have a capable gardening staff. Others make lace when they can afford to buy yards of it. You bake."

"You truly don't mind?" Ivy pressed.

He smiled, dipping his spoon into the soup. "Not so long as I can enjoy the product of your labor."

Ivy sagged, shoulders lighter than they had been in weeks. "Oh, Kendall, I'm so glad. And Mrs. Sheppard and I never meant to cheat anyone. We weren't sure you would want me to bake for Miss Thorn's wedding, as the dowager duchess requested. I suspect those supplies are the ones Mrs. Sheppard was trying to hide."

"Mystery solved, then," he said. "Please let her know she has no need for concern. But I stand by my assessment. The greater discrepancy came long before you started baking at Villa Romanesque. The oddity stopped when I went to London. At first, I thought the change had something to do with my absence. Then I realized I wasn't the only one absent. Sir Alexander was in America during that time."

Ivy stared at him. "Then he truly did steal from the estate."

Kendall nodded. "We are well rid of him."

The soup had never tasted finer. She was so relieved to have her baking out in the open and the solicitor out of their lives, she had finished the soup and the salmon that followed before she remembered they had other important matters to discuss.

But Kendall did nothing to deepen the conversation, asking after Sophia and Petunia, offering suggestions for the rest of the summer. He even broached the possibility of a house party at Christmas.

"Sophia and I would enjoy having all our family close," he said, gaze on hers.

Their family. The thought that he had embraced all the

Batemans made her so happy that she almost forgot again. She straightened her shoulders, determined to bring up the subject herself when Travis cleared away the dishes.

But before she could open her mouth, the footman returned with Mrs. Sheppard, each carrying a covered platter.

"What's this?" Ivy asked, glancing between the silver domes. The housekeeper sent her a smile of encouragement before she and Travis withdrew.

"Open that one first," Kendall said with a nod to the one on the right of her.

Ivy lifted the lid. On the white porcelain platter inside lay a dozen Naples biscuits, the edges just a bit too brown. The scent of rosewater floated up from them.

She frowned. "I didn't bake these."

"No," he said. "I did. I wanted to show you how much I value you, Ivy. It is clear to me that one of the ways you show your love for others is to bake for them."

He was right. She baked for the love of her family. But did that mean…?

He nodded to the other silver cover. "Now that one."

Hand trembling once more, Ivy did as he bid.

The diamond necklace and tiara inside glittered in the light, sending rainbows flashing across the white tablecloth. Ivy drew in a breath.

Kendall rose and came around the table. "These were my mother's. She told my father to instruct me to give them to my wife."

He went down on one knee beside Ivy. "My darling Ivy, who made me believe in love again, will you be my wife, in every sense of that word?"

Ivy stared into his face, so much dearer now than the day he'd first proposed. She knew the warmth in those dark eyes, the silken brush of his mustache. She'd felt the strength in his arms, heard the love in his voice when he spoke to Sophia. She'd worked and hoped and prayed for this moment, the moment she could truly call him husband.

"Yes, Kendall," she said, never surer of herself. "I love you so much. I've been trying to find a way to ask you to change our agreement. I want to be your wife, your true wife."

He straightened and opened his arms, and she stepped into them, wrapping her arms about his waist. Cradled close, his lips brushing hers, she knew that no Roman artifact would ever be finer, no cinnamon bun sweeter, than the love she shared with this man.

He pulled back with a smile. "I feel as if I should arrange a wedding, attend a dozen betrothal balls."

"No need," Ivy assured him. "We have been acting as husband and wife for weeks. This is just the next step on our journey together."

He reached out to hold her hand, as if he relished the touch as much as she did. "And what does that next step entail?"

Was he teasing her? Even though she had every right to tell him what she wanted, her cheeks were heating. "Now we share everything."

He regarded their joined hands. "Everything? I know some husbands and wives who do not share a bedchamber."

Ivy frowned. "Why? It's terribly inconvenient for the staff."

He barked out a laugh, then pulled her close once more. "Well, I certainly wouldn't want to inconvenience the staff, or my wife."

His wife. Ivy cuddled against him, joy and wonder mixing like yeast in dough and raising her spirits, her hopes. Past his shoulder, she spotted Mrs. Sheppard and Travis peeking at them from around a statue. The housekeeper gave her a thumbs up before they disappeared.

"Perhaps I'll enlarge the kitchen," Kendall said against her hair. "Build one of those Rumford ranges Mrs. Sheppard was enthusiastic about. And Sophia will need a suite of rooms redecorated just for her so you and I can share the suite."

"Kendall, the expense!" Ivy protested, pulling back.

He touched her cheek with gentle fingers. "My darling, we are not poor. Far from it. Allow me to spoil you."

"I have been quite spoiled enough," Ivy informed him. "There's no need to expand the house. Villa Romanesque is beautiful just as it is. Tomorrow, we can stroll through the rooms, pick out which ones are better suited for our purposes."

Something warm gathered in his dark eyes. "And tonight?"

"Tonight and every night to come, I plan to spend with my husband," Ivy said. "Why do you think I married a marquess?"

EPILOGUE

Meredith and Julian married a fortnight later, on a brilliant summer morning, at the castle of the Duke and Duchess of Wey. Their distinguished guests sat on gilded chairs in the vast hall, while Meredith in the lavender lace gown Lydia and Charlotte had helped her choose took her vows with Julian under a canopy of hot house roses provided by the Earl of Carrolton. And when Julian looked into her eyes and promised to love her for as long as they both should live, she knew their love would last long beyond that. She wasn't sure her feet hit the ground as they walked back through the crowd to usher their friends into the formal garden at the back of the castle, where the cakes and biscuits Lord Kendall's marvelous new baker had provided were arranged with other dishes on damask-draped tables.

"You make a lovely bride," Daisy Bateman said as her family came through the receiving line.

"You will have your turn," Charlotte reminded her, arm entwined with Sir Matthew's.

The Batemans were staying with Ivy and Lord Kendall, who couldn't look happier. It seemed their marriage of convenience had become much more. In fact, she noticed, glancing around the flower-scented garden, all her clients looked singularly happy.

Jane and His Grace held hands as they helped their

daughters select treats from the loaded tables. Patience sat on a swing under a tree while Sir Harry pushed her, grinning. The pretty blonde had already told Meredith that she was expecting a baby. So was Yvette. The Frenchwoman and her gentle giant of a husband, the earl, were discussing the possibilities of requesting cuttings of some of the plants for his own botanical studies. Beyond them, the always bubbly Lydia and her brilliant husband, Viscount Worthington, were debating the efficacy of hot air over hydrogen in balloons with, of all people, the dowager duchess of Wey and the dowager countess of Carrolton, who were good friends.

Just as pleasing, Sir Alexander Prentice was out of their lives. After she, Julian, and Lord Kendall had confronted the solicitor, Mr. Cowls had related that Sir Alexander had been chosen to tend to Crown business in the wilds of Canada. She was certain Julian and the prince had had something to do with that. She would likely never see the solicitor again.

She and Julian finished thanking the last of their guests, and she turned from the receiving line to the garden with a sigh. "Weddings bring out the best in people."

"Especially people in love," Julian agreed, offering her his arm. She accepted it, and they set out to promenade on the graveled path.

A castle footman approached with Fortune on a leash. While Meredith would have loved to have her pet beside her during her vows, the local vicar had been so shocked by the suggestion, she had agreed to allow Fortune to watch from the gallery. Now she picked up her pet a moment, held her close.

"We did it," she whispered. "All of them settled and all of them happy. Even Julian and me."

Fortune's tail swished back and forth as if she had never doubted the matter.

Julian smiled as she lowered the cat to the ground and

allowed her to run before them, secure on the leash. Then he turned to her, eyes intent, as if he wasn't sure of her. What was this?

"Meredith," he said, "you have made me the happiest of men. I hope you will accept a wedding present from me." He reached into the pocket of his dove grey wedding coat, pulled out a brass key, and held it out to her.

Meredith frowned at it, memories tugging. But it couldn't be. She glanced up to meet his gaze. "Is that...?" The name of her childhood home stuck in her throat, as if afraid it would be taken from her as well.

"The key to Rose Hill," he said, wrapping his hand around hers, pressing the heavy brass against her fingers. "It seems your cousin did not find it to his liking after all. He was persuaded to sell to me."

The beautiful garden grew misty as tears filled her eyes. "But I thought it had to go to a male heir."

"Your grandfather set up his will that way," he allowed. "Your cousin Nigel had no such requirements. It was a legal matter that could be rectified in this case." He wiggled his brows at her. "I am a solicitor, you know."

She clung to his hand, scarcely able to believe what he'd done for her. "Oh, Julian, you've given me back my home."

"Our home," he corrected her, releasing her hand to wrap his arms about her. "I still remember how you proposed to me under the kissing bough that Christmas. I look forward to making many more memories there together." He leaned back to grin at her. "Perhaps Lord Kendall's baker can show your cook how to make brambleberry pie as good as your mother's."

She kissed him then, heart so full she would not have been surprised if it overflowed the island to meet the Thames.

"We are blessed," she murmured, leaning back. "You are a rising favorite with the prince. Your work is respected by all."

"As is yours," he assured her.

Fortune's tug on the leash reminded her they were supposed to be strolling. Yet the sunshine of her happiness dimmed just the slightest as they started out again. "Even if I appear to be finished. I haven't located another lady requiring my aid in weeks."

"Perhaps you should expand beyond gentlewomen," Julian suggested, turning her past the high castle wall. "They aren't the only ones in need of respectable positions."

Meredith frowned. "To whom do you refer?"

"What about the gentlemen?" he asked. "Second sons traditionally have a difficult time finding their place in the scheme of things. Widowers can be isolated. Those on the cusp of Society—solicitors, architects, engineers— need assistance from time to time. Think of Lord Kendall's brother. Lord Weston will return from duty at some point. He'd likely rather find useful ways to fill his time than sit around and watch his brother and bride bill and coo."

Fortune scampered back to them and rubbed herself against Julian's stockings as if endorsing the idea.

"Gentlemen," Meredith mused. "What an intriguing thought."

Julian stopped and put his arms about her. "Something to be considered in more depth another day. I've been waiting ten years to call us husband and wife. I'm sure Fortune would tell you it's high time we thought of our own romance."

Fortune mewed as if she quite agreed. Then she turned her back to give them a moment of privacy and fixed her great copper eyes on the future.

Dear Reader
    Thank you for choosing Ivy and Kendall's story. If this is the first book you've read in the Fortune's Brides series, you may want to look for the others: *Never Doubt a Duke, Never Borrow a Baronet, Never Envy an Earl, Never Vie for a Viscount,* and *Never Kneel to a Knight.* If you have read all those, thank you for following Fortune and Meredith's adventures as they helped gentlewomen down on their luck find homes. After all, only a matchmaking cat can hunt true love.

    If you enjoyed this book, there are several things you could do now:

    Sign up for a free e-mail alert at http://eepurl.com/baqwVT so you'll be the first to know whenever a new book is out or on sale. I offer exclusive free short stories to my subscribers from time to time. Don't miss out.

    Post a review on a bookseller site or Goodreads to help others find the book.

    Discover my many other books on my website at *www.reginascott.com.*

    Blessings!

Regina Scott

OTHER BOOKS BY REGINA SCOTT

Spy Matchmaker Series
The Husband Mission
The June Bride Conspiracy
The Heiress Objective

Perfection

And other books for Love Inspired Historical and
Timeless Regency collections.

ABOUT THE AUTHOR

R egina Scott started writing novels in the third grade. Thankfully for literature as we know it, she didn't sell her first novel until she learned a bit more about writing. Since her first book was published, her stories have traveled the globe, with translations in many languages including Dutch, German, Italian, and Portuguese. She now has more than forty-five published works of warm, witty romance.

Unlike Ivy, she has no skill for baking. Her cupcakes are shaped more like craters, and she's twice managed to melt a spatula into the food she was cooking. Her oldest son, however, is an accomplished chef, and her critique partner and dear friend, Kristy J. Manhattan, is an excellent cook. Kristy helped Regina come up with the idea for Fortune's Brides. She is an avid fan of cats, supporting spay and neuter clinics and pet rescue groups. If Fortune resembles any cat you know, credit Kristy.

Regina Scott and her husband of 30 years reside in the Puget Sound area of Washington State on the way to Mt. Rainier. She has dressed as a Regency dandy, driven four-in-hand, and sailed on a tall ship, all in the name of research, of course. Learn more about her at her website at *www.reginascott.com.*